RUDYARD KIPLING'S

THE JUNGLE BOOK

STONE ARCH BOOKS
MINNEAPOLIS   SAN DIEGO

RUDYARD KIPLING'S THE JUNGLE BOOK

RETOLD BY **CARL BOWEN**

ILLUSTRATED BY **GERARDO SANDOVAL**

COLORED BY **BENNY FUENTES**

DESIGNER: **BRANN GARVEY**

EDITOR: **DONALD LEMKE**

ASSOC. EDITOR: **SEAN TULIEN**

ART DIRECTOR: **BOB LENTZ**

CREATIVE DIRECTOR: **HEATHER KINDSETH**

EDITORIAL DIRECTOR: **MICHAEL DAHL**

Graphic Revolve is published by Stone Arch Books 151 Good Counsel Drive, P.O. Box 669 Mankato, Minnesota 56002 www.stonearchbooks.com Copyright © 2010 by Stone Arch Books All rights reserved. No part of this publication may be reproduced in whole or in part, or stored in a retrieval system, or transmitted in any form or by any means, electronic, mechanical, photocopying, recording, or otherwise, without written permission of the publisher.

Library of Congress Cataloging-in-Publication Data
Bowen, Carl.
  The jungle book / by Rudyard Kipling ; retold by Carl Bowen ; illustrated by Gerardo Sandoval.
    p. cm. -- (Graphic revolve)
  ISBN 978-1-4342-1584-0 (library binding) -- ISBN 978-1-4342-1739-4 (pbk.)
  1. Graphic novels. [1. Graphic novels. 2. Jungles--Fiction. 3. Animals--Fiction. 4. India--Fiction.] I. Sandoval, Gerardo, 1974- ill. II. Kipling, Rudyard, 1865-1936. Jungle book. III. Title.
  PZ7.7.B69Ju 2010
   741.5'973--dc22   2009013683

Summary: In the jungles of India, a pack of wolves discovers a young boy. They name the boy Mowgli and protect him against dangers, including Shere Kan, the most savage tiger in the jungle. As Mowgli grows up, he learns the ways of the jungle from Bagheera the panther, the wise bear, Baloo, and other animals. Soon, he must decide whether to remain among beasts or embrace his own kind.

Printed in the United States of America

CONTENTS

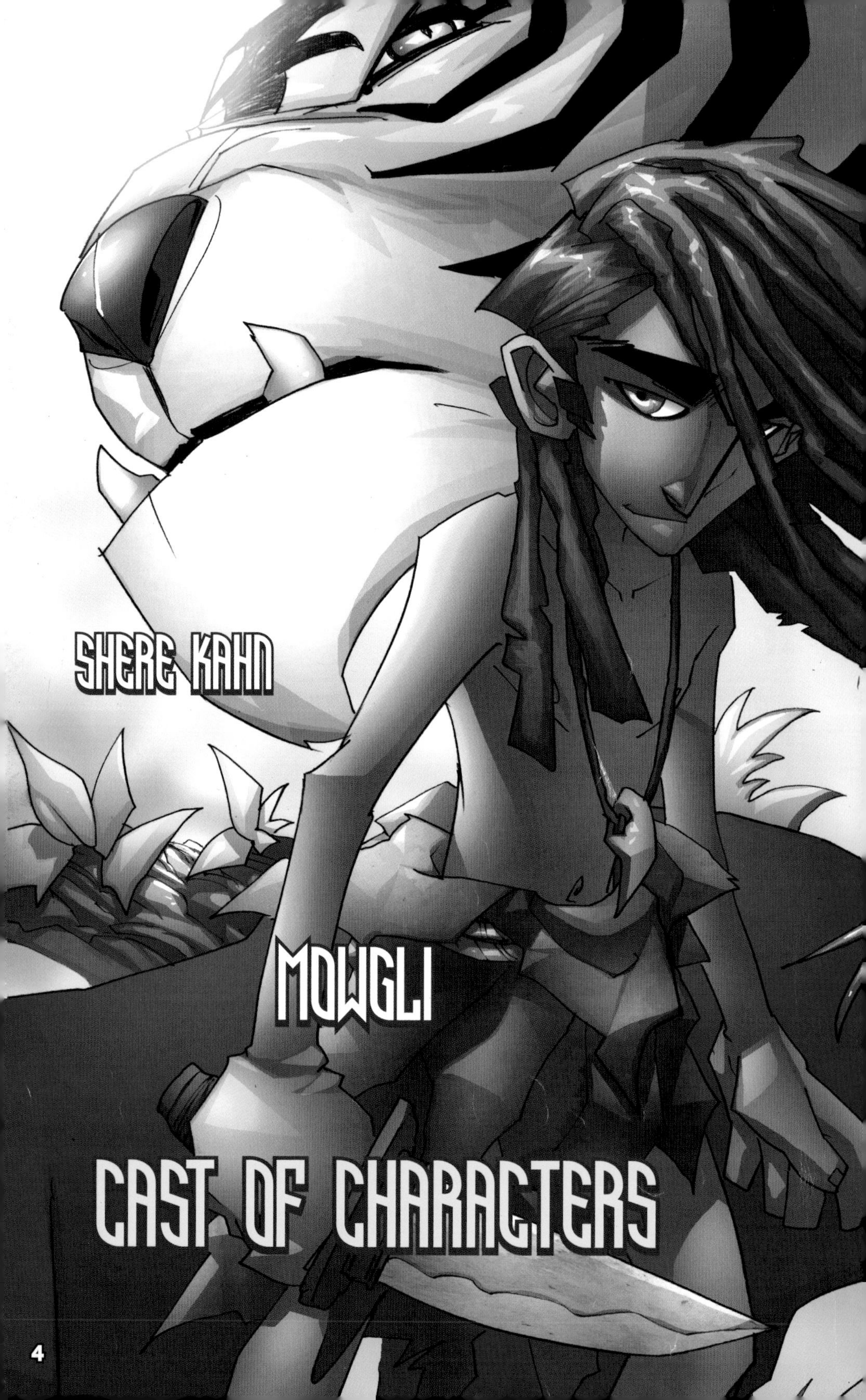
SHERE KAHN
MOWGLI
CAST OF CHARACTERS

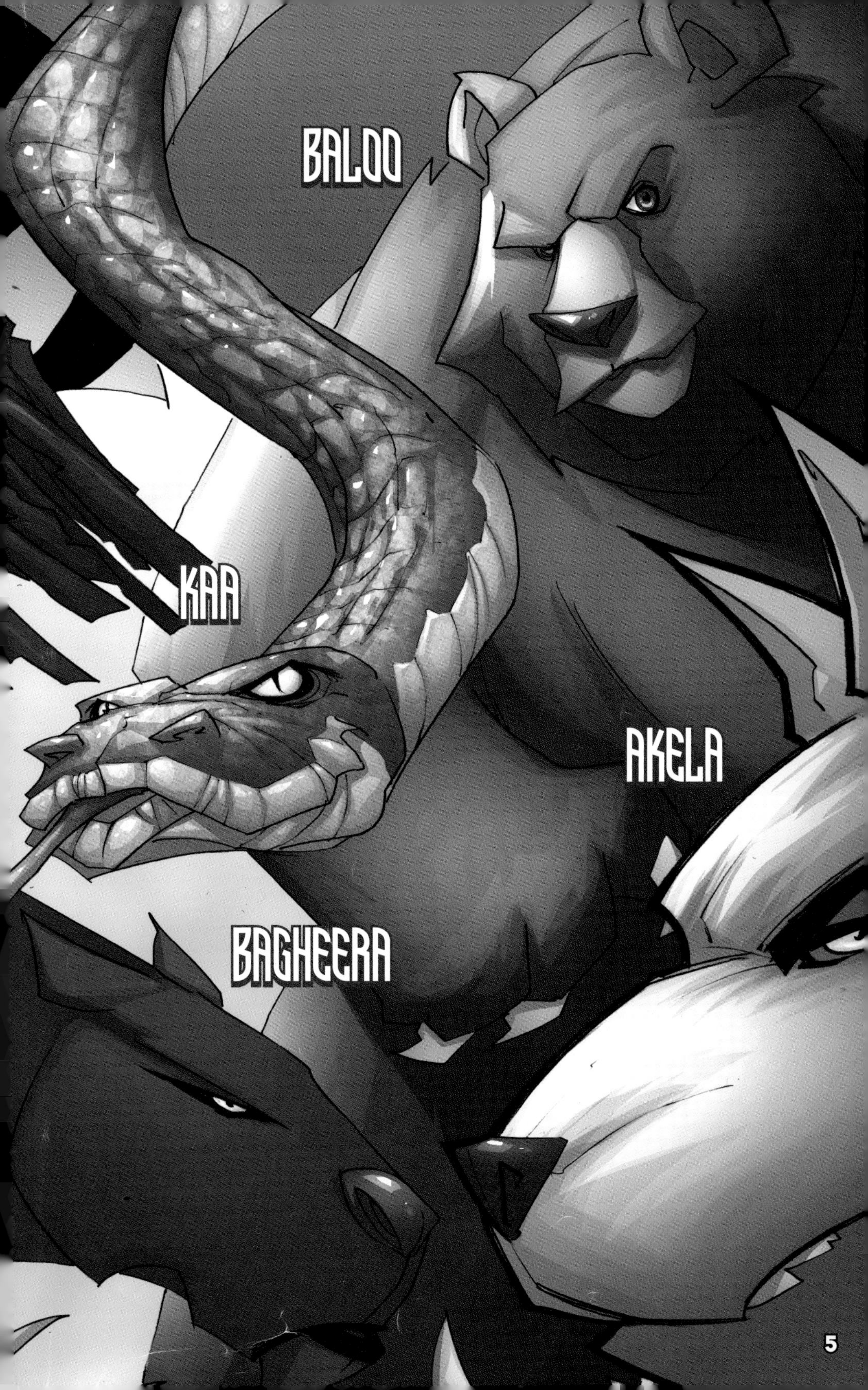
BALOO
KAA
AKELA
BAGHEERA

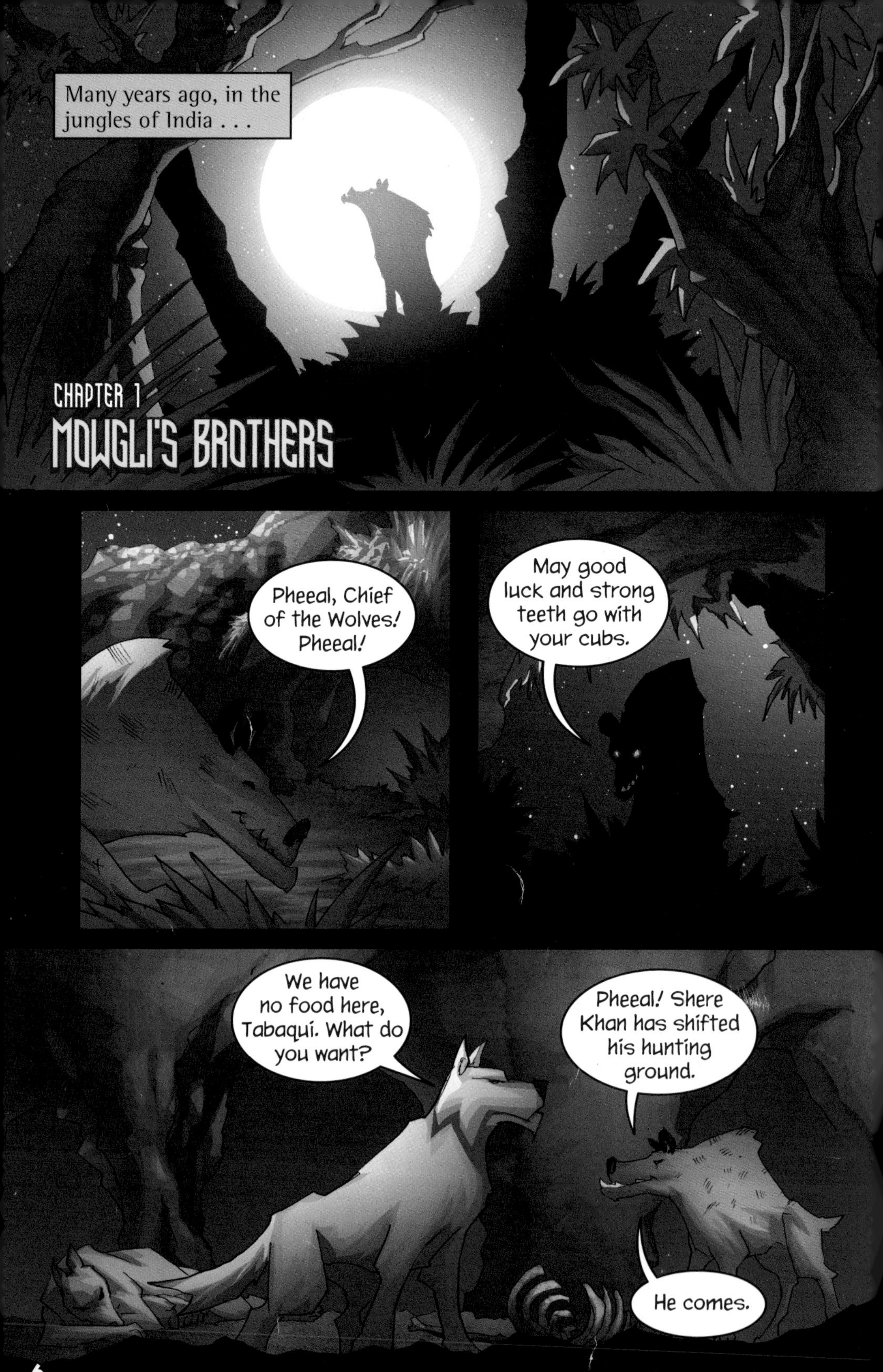
Many years ago, in the jungles of India . . .
CHAPTER 1
MOWGLI'S BROTHERS
Pheeal, Chief of the Wolves! Pheeal!
May good luck and strong teeth go with your cubs.
We have no food here, Tabaqui. What do you want?
Pheeal! Shere Khan has shifted his hunting ground.
He comes.

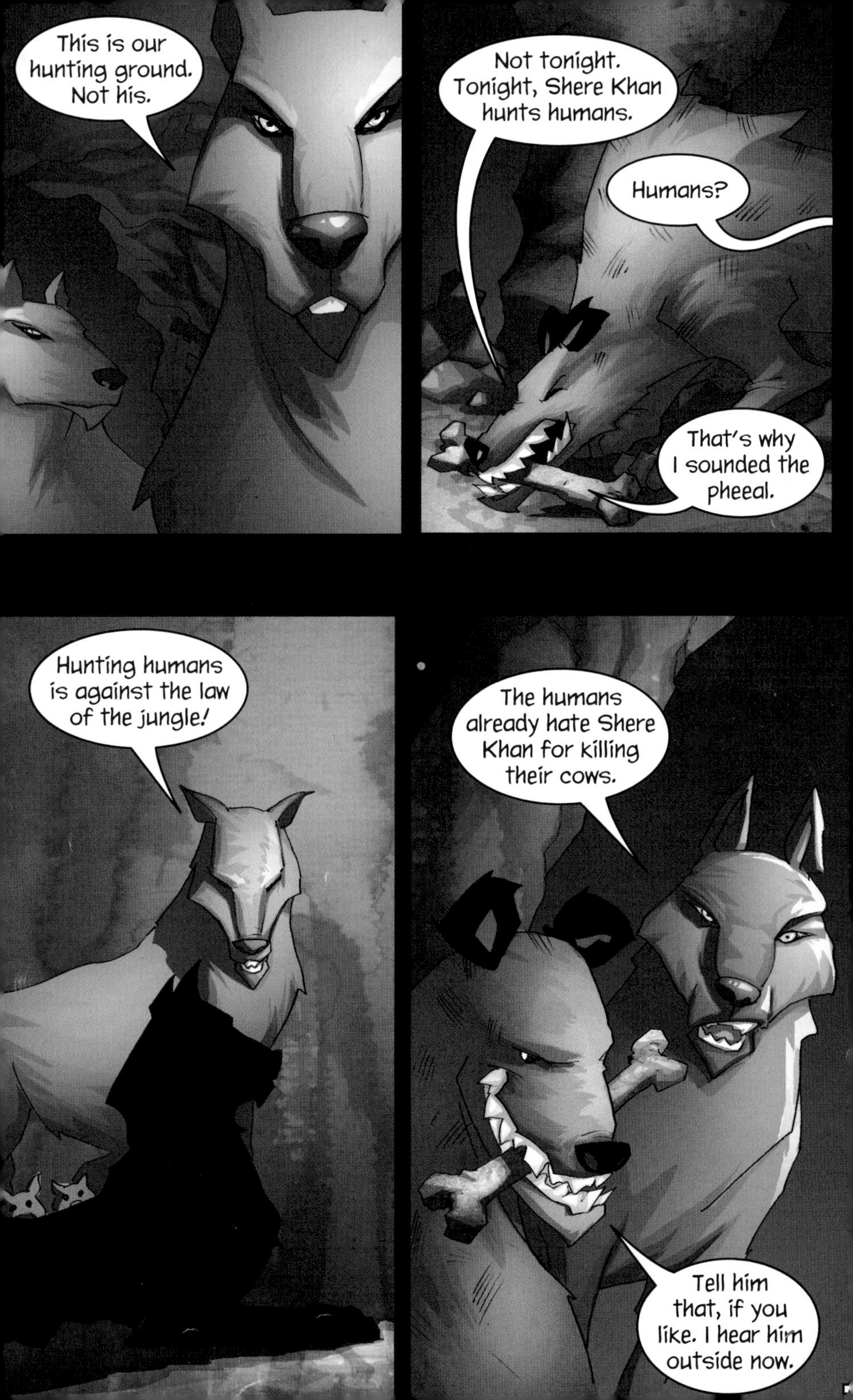
This is our hunting ground. Not his.
Not tonight. Tonight, Shere Khan hunts humans.
Humans?
That's why I sounded the pheeal.
Hunting humans is against the law of the jungle!
The humans already hate Shere Khan for killing their cows.
Tell him that, if you like. I hear him outside now.

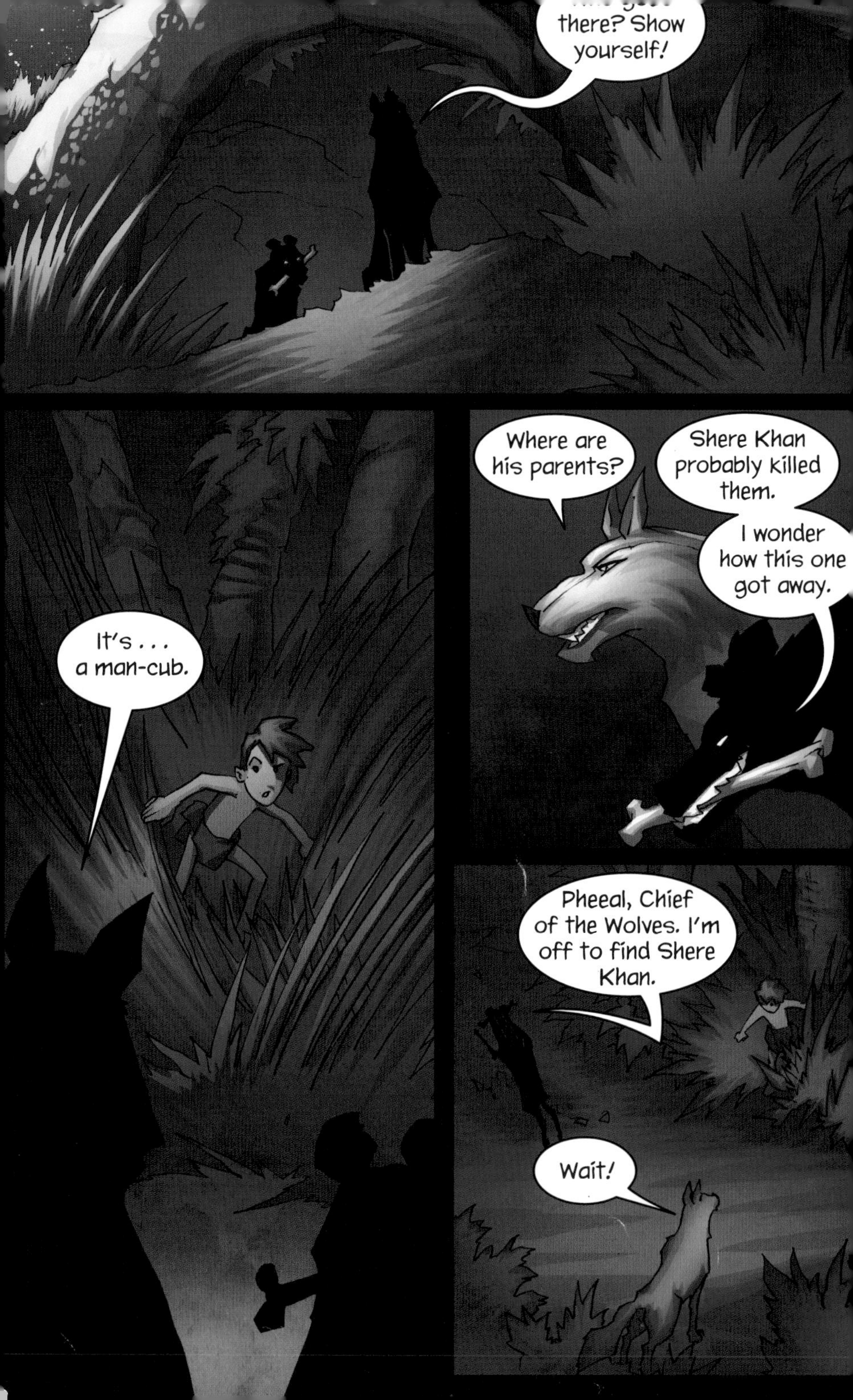
there? Show yourself!
It's . . . a man-cub.
Where are his parents?
Shere Khan probably killed them.
I wonder how this one got away.
Pheeal, Chief of the Wolves. I'm off to find Shere Khan.
Wait!

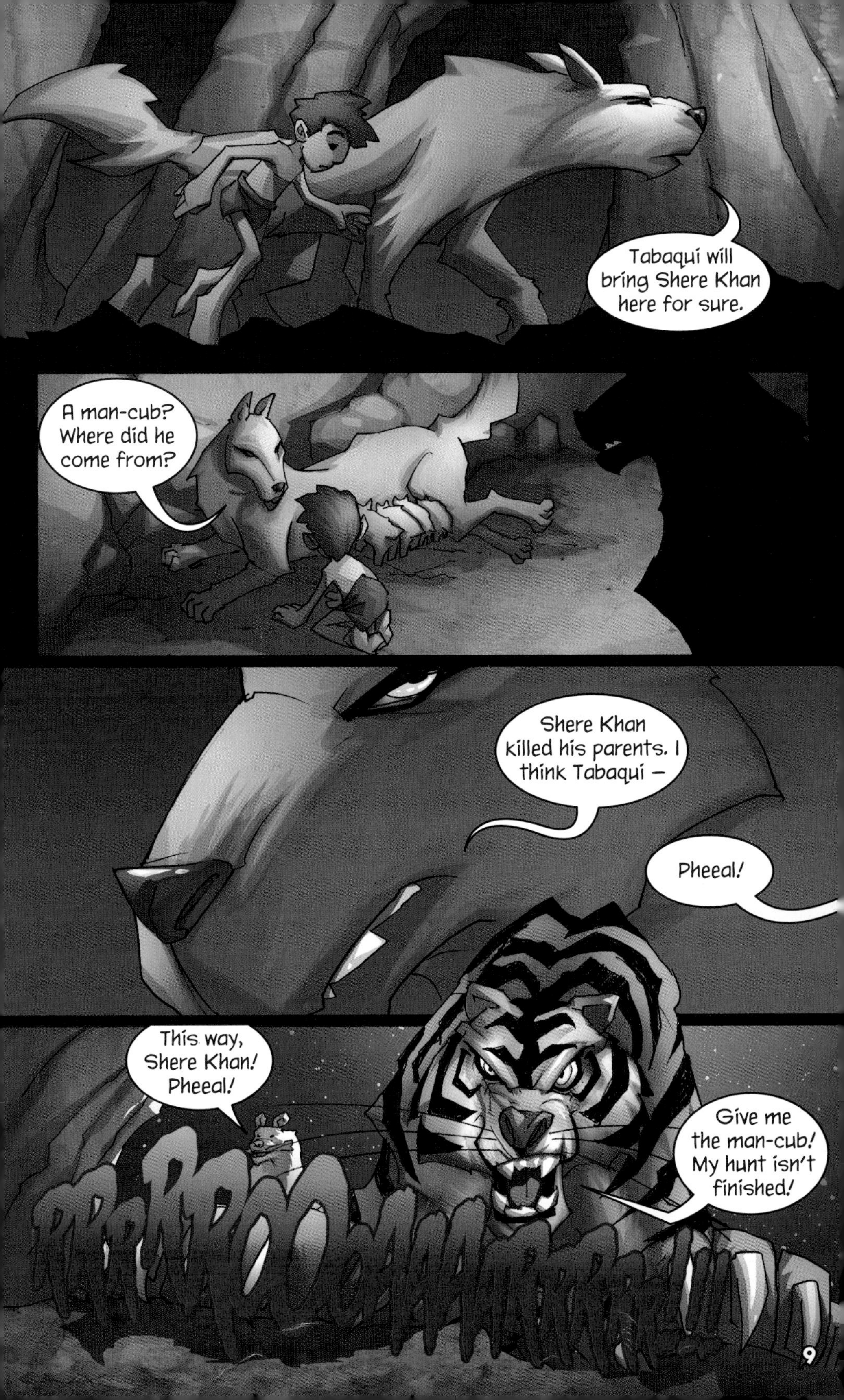
Tabaqui will bring Shere Khan here for sure.
A man-cub? Where did he come from?
Shere Khan killed his parents. I think Tabaqui —
Pheeal!
This way, Shere Khan! Pheeal!
Give me the man-cub! My hunt isn't finished!
RRRROOOAAARRRR!

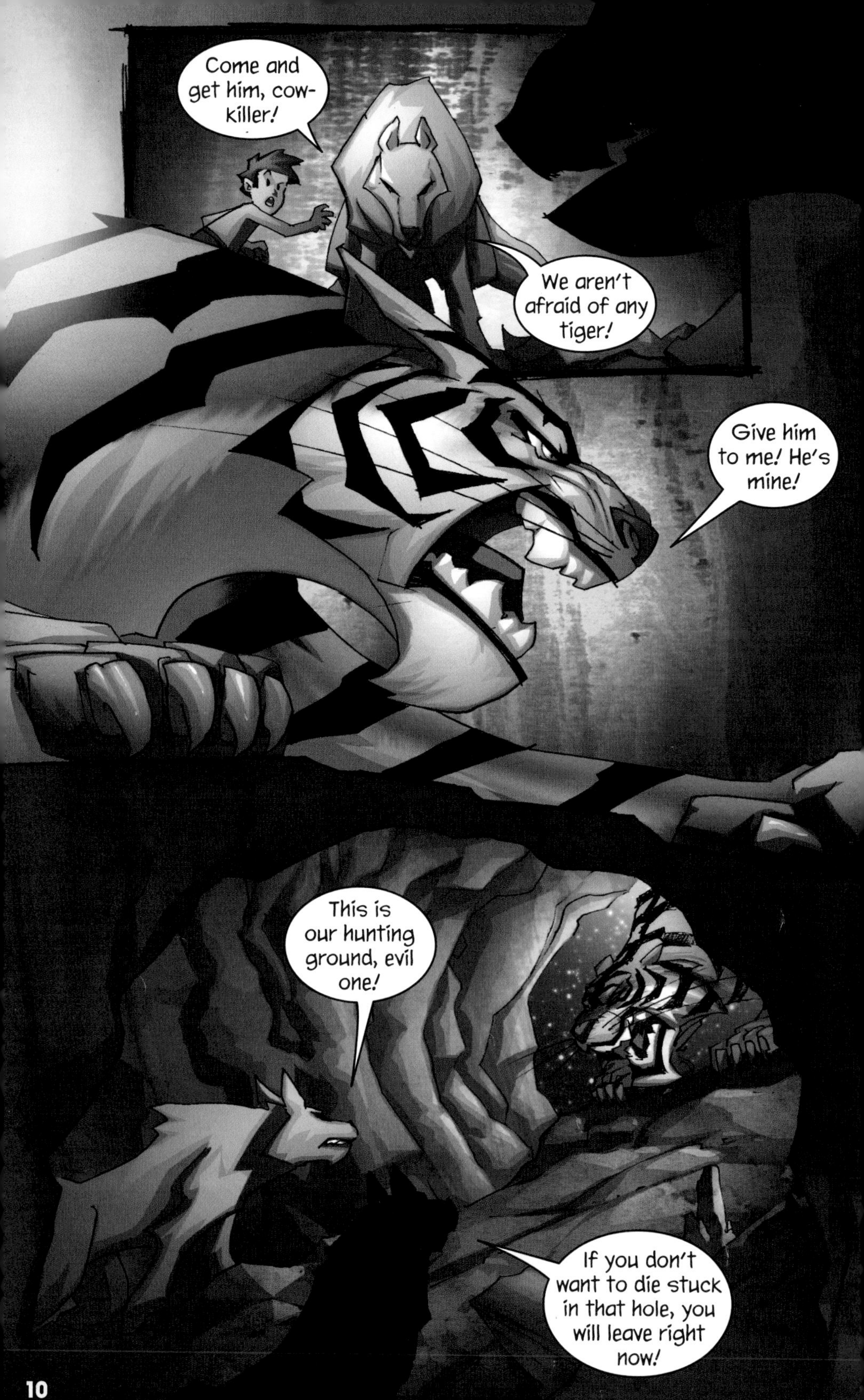
Come and get him, cow-killer!
We aren't afraid of any tiger!
Give him to me! He's mine!
This is our hunting ground, evil one!
If you don't want to die stuck in that hole, you will leave right now!

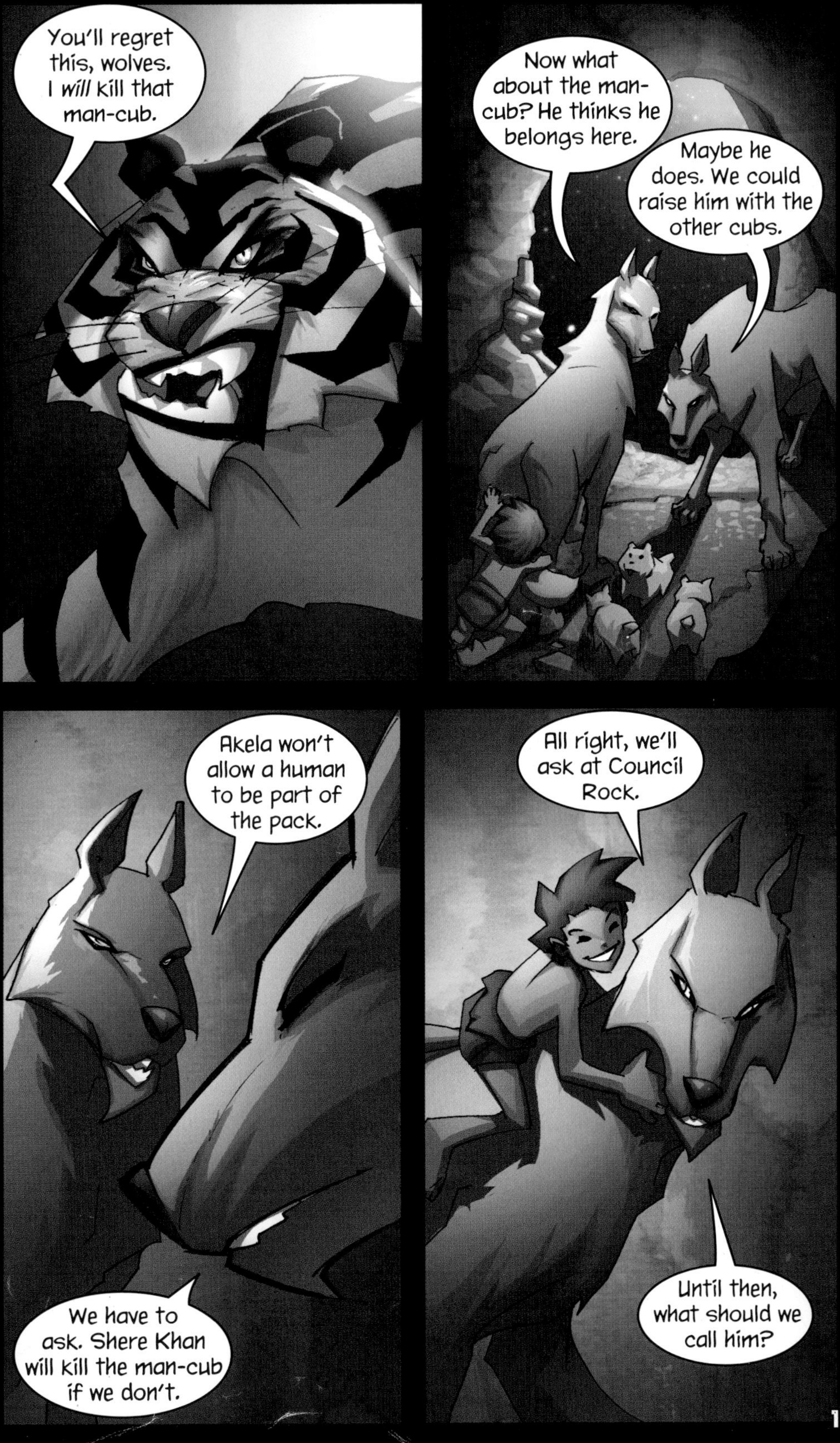
You'll regret this, wolves. I *will* kill that man-cub.
Now what about the man-cub? He thinks he belongs here.
Maybe he does. We could raise him with the other cubs.
Akela won't allow a human to be part of the pack.
We have to ask. Shere Khan will kill the man-cub if we don't.
All right, we'll ask at Council Rock.
Until then, what should we call him?

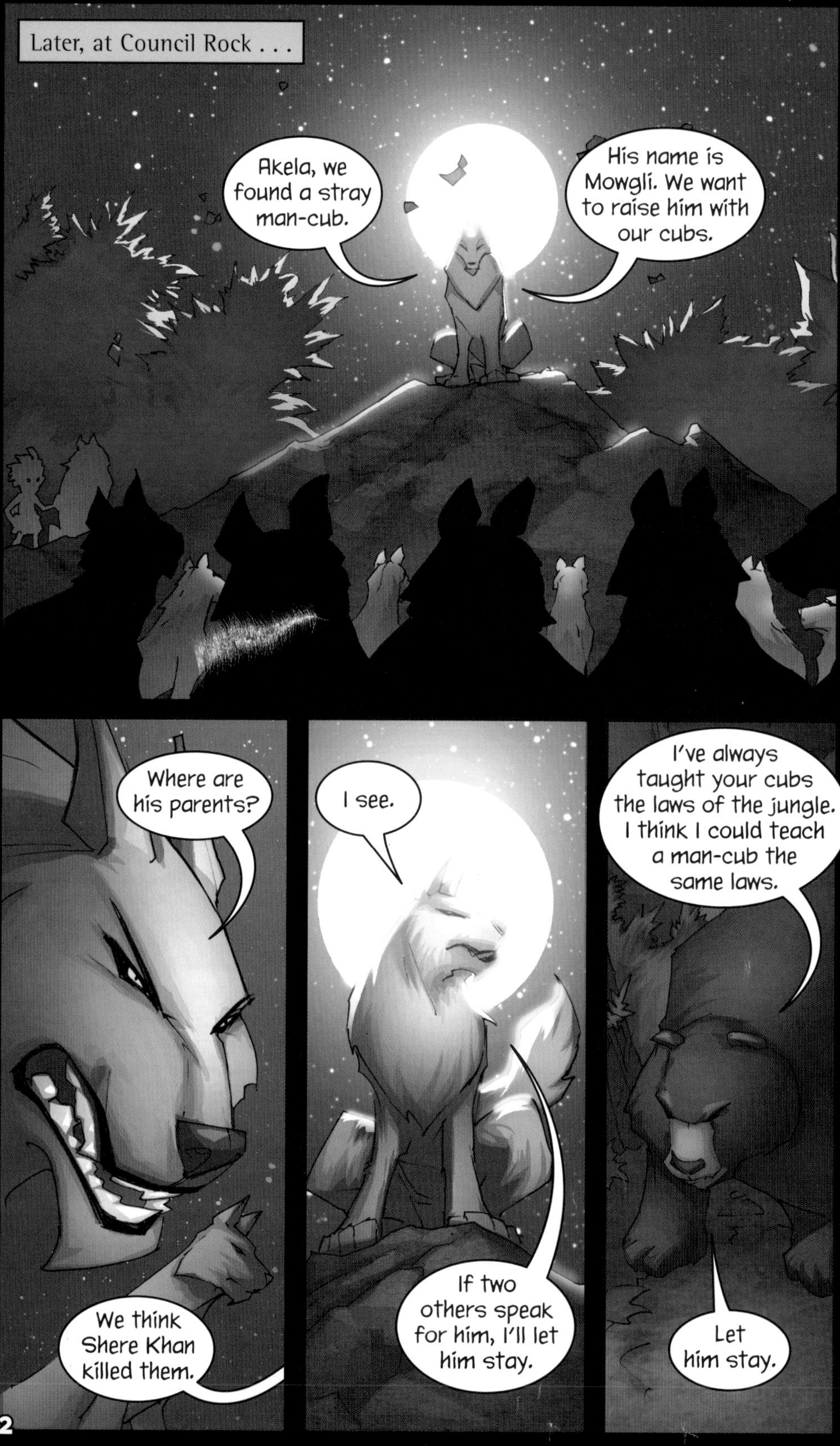

Later, at Council Rock . . .
Akela, we found a stray man-cub.
His name is Mowgli. We want to raise him with our cubs.
Where are his parents?
We think Shere Khan killed them.
I see.
If two others speak for him, I'll let him stay.
I've always taught your cubs the laws of the jungle. I think I could teach a man-cub the same laws.
Let him stay.

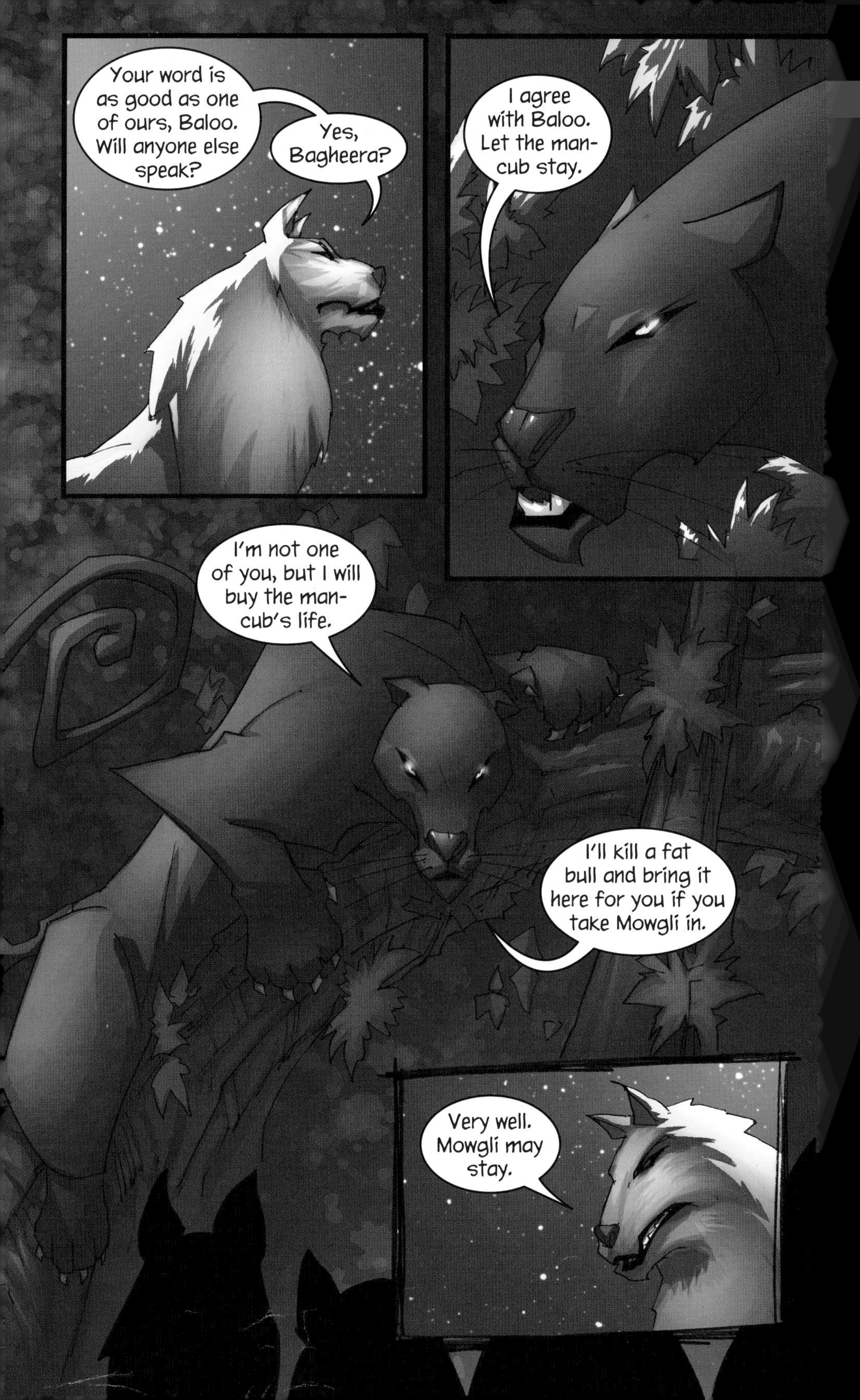
Your word is as good as one of ours, Baloo. Will anyone else speak?
Yes, Bagheera?
I agree with Baloo. Let the man-cub stay.
I'm not one of you, but I will buy the man-cub's life.
I'll kill a fat bull and bring it here for you if you take Mowgli in.
Very well. Mowgli may stay.

CHAPTER 2
KAA'S HUNTING

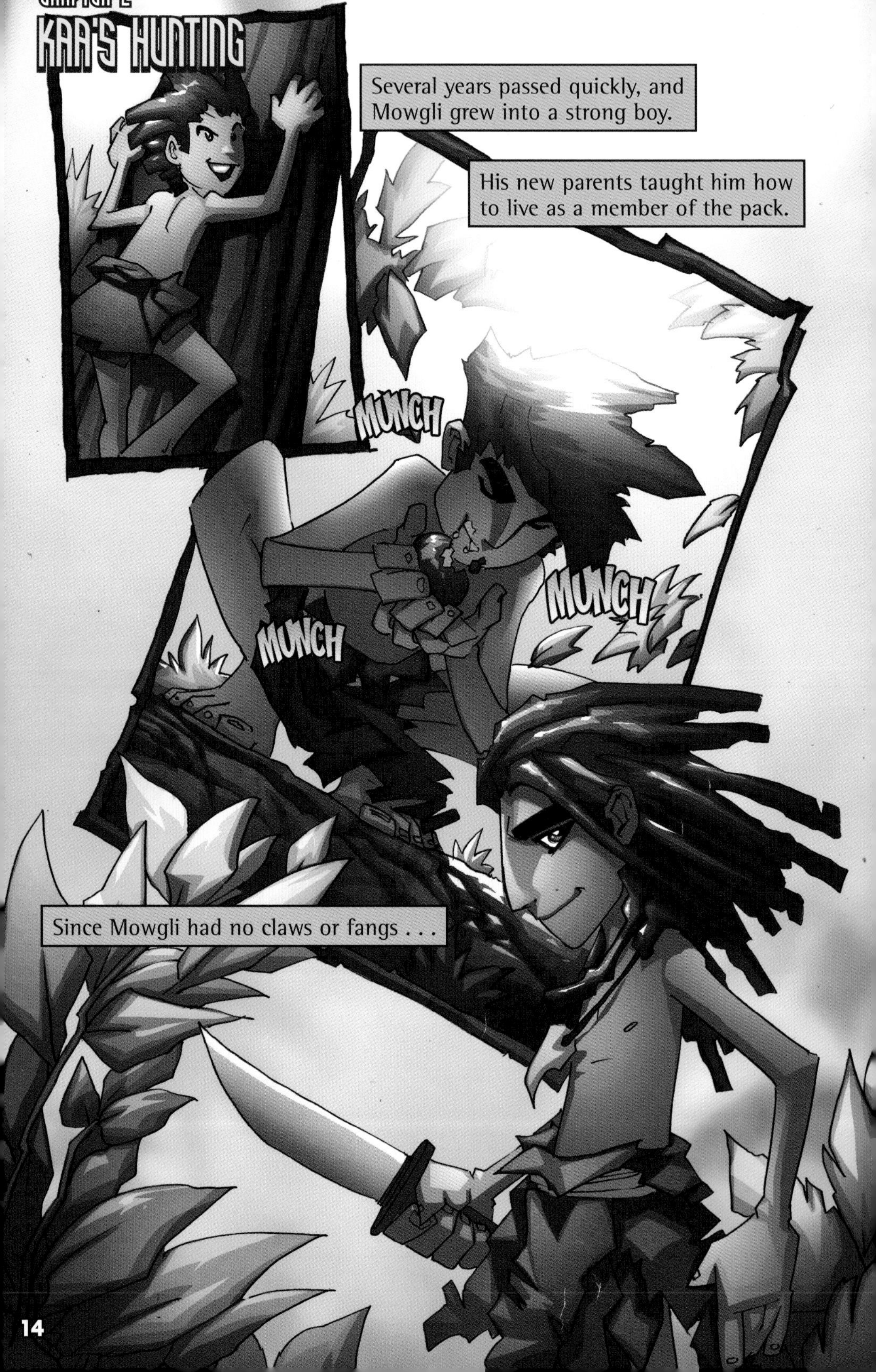
Several years passed quickly, and Mowgli grew into a strong boy.
His new parents taught him how to live as a member of the pack.
MUNCH
MUNCH
MUNCH
Since Mowgli had no claws or fangs . . .

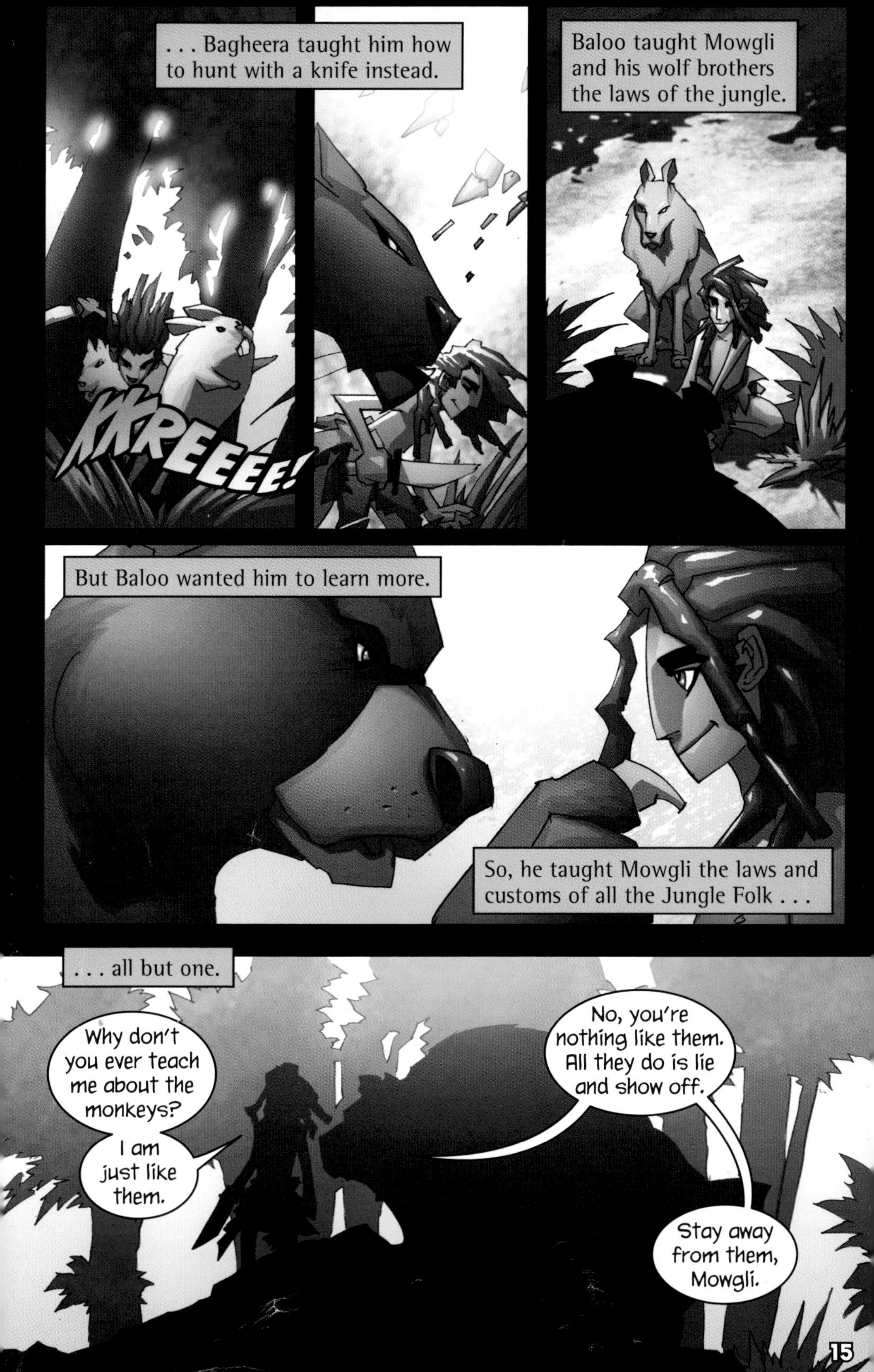
. . . Bagheera taught him how to hunt with a knife instead.
KKREEEEE!
Baloo taught Mowgli and his wolf brothers the laws of the jungle.
But Baloo wanted him to learn more.
So, he taught Mowgli the laws and customs of all the Jungle Folk . . .
. . . all but one.
Why don't you ever teach me about the monkeys?
I am just like them.
No, you're nothing like them. All they do is lie and show off.
Stay away from them, Mowgli.

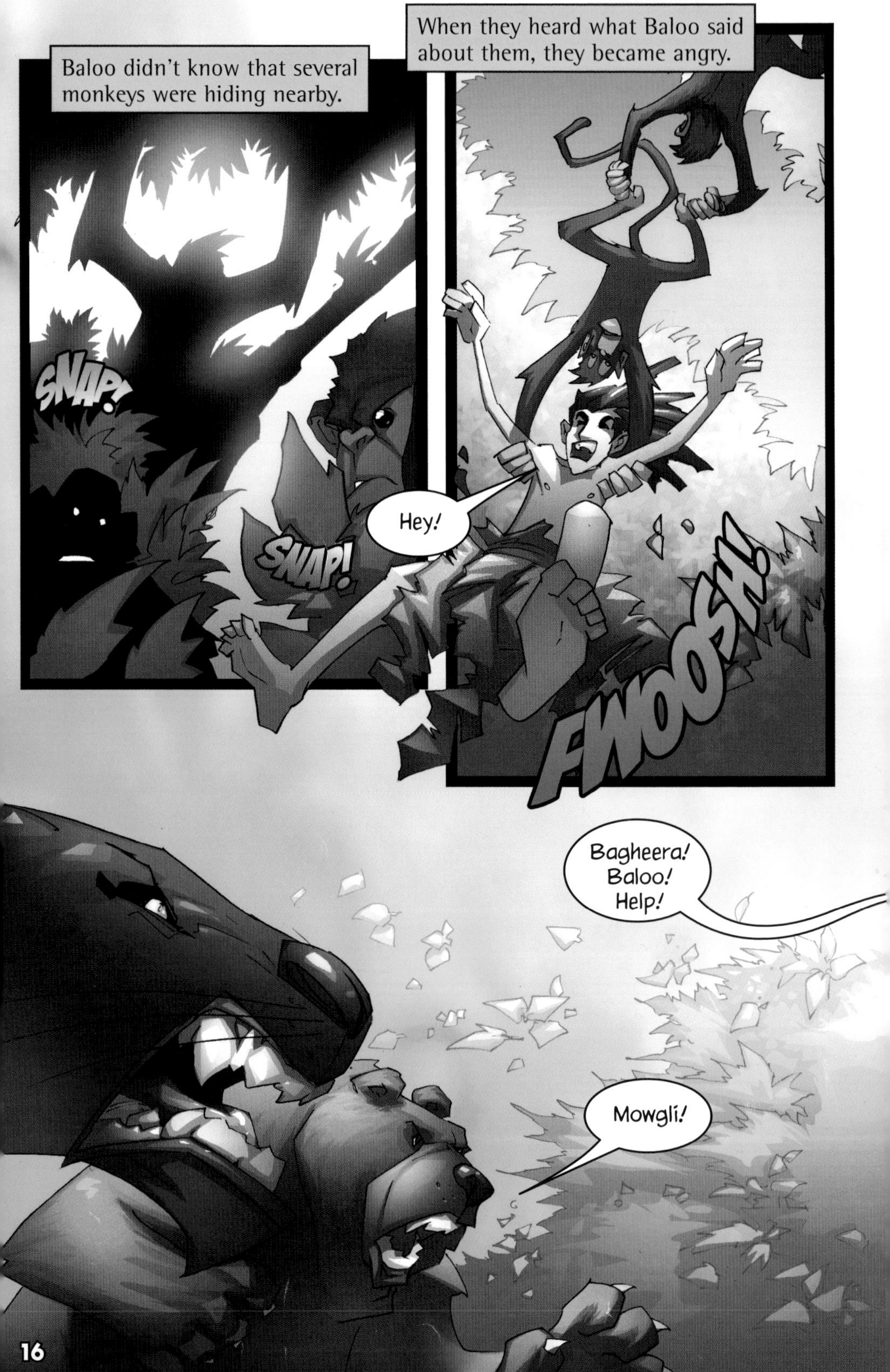
Baloo didn't know that several monkeys were hiding nearby.
SNAP!
SNAP!
When they heard what Baloo said about them, they became angry.
Hey!
FWOOSH!
Bagheera! Baloo! Help!
Mowgli!

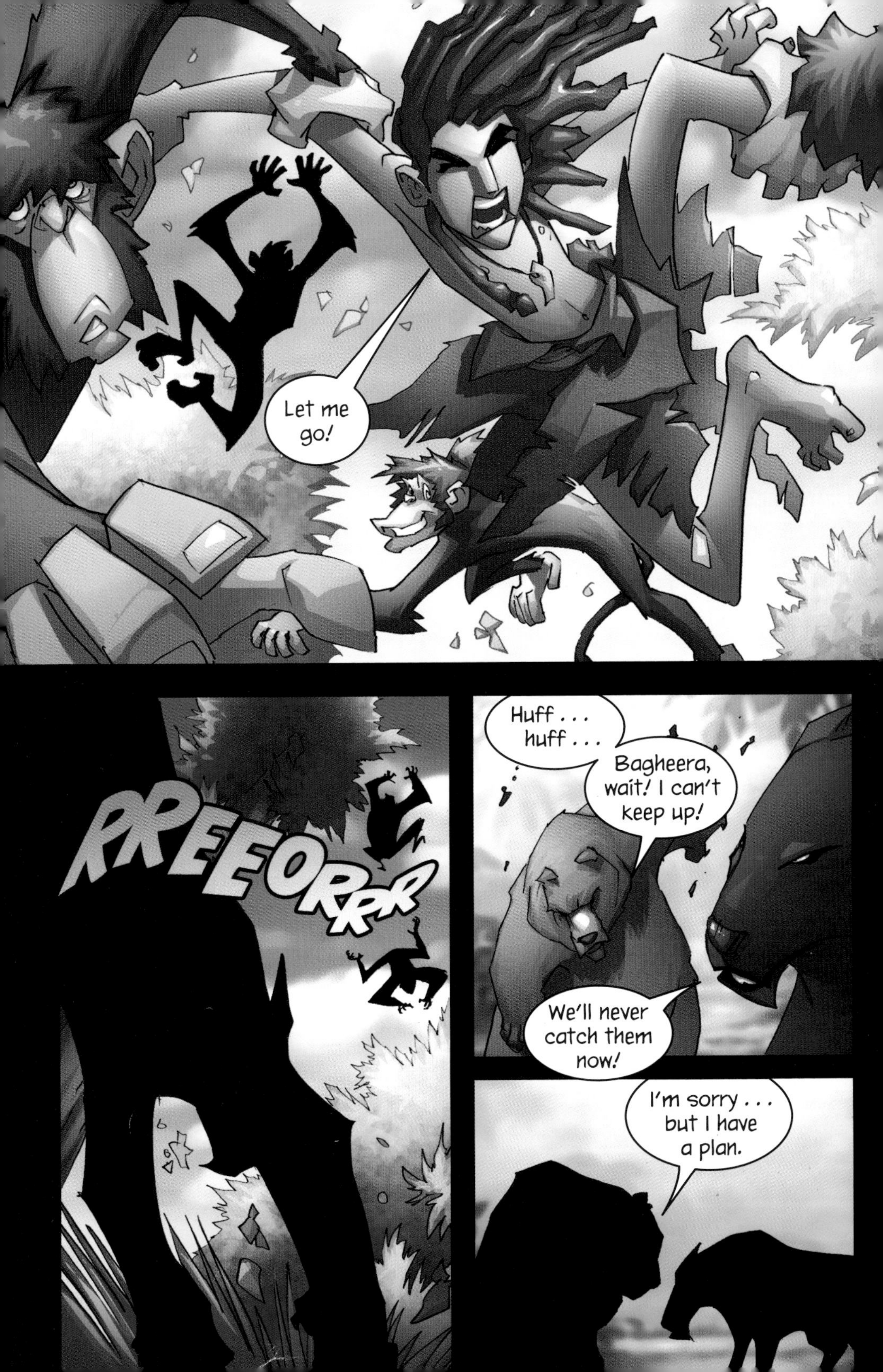
Let me go!
REEEORRR
Huff . . . huff . . .
Bagheera, wait! I can't keep up!
We'll never catch them now!
I'm sorry . . . but I have a plan.

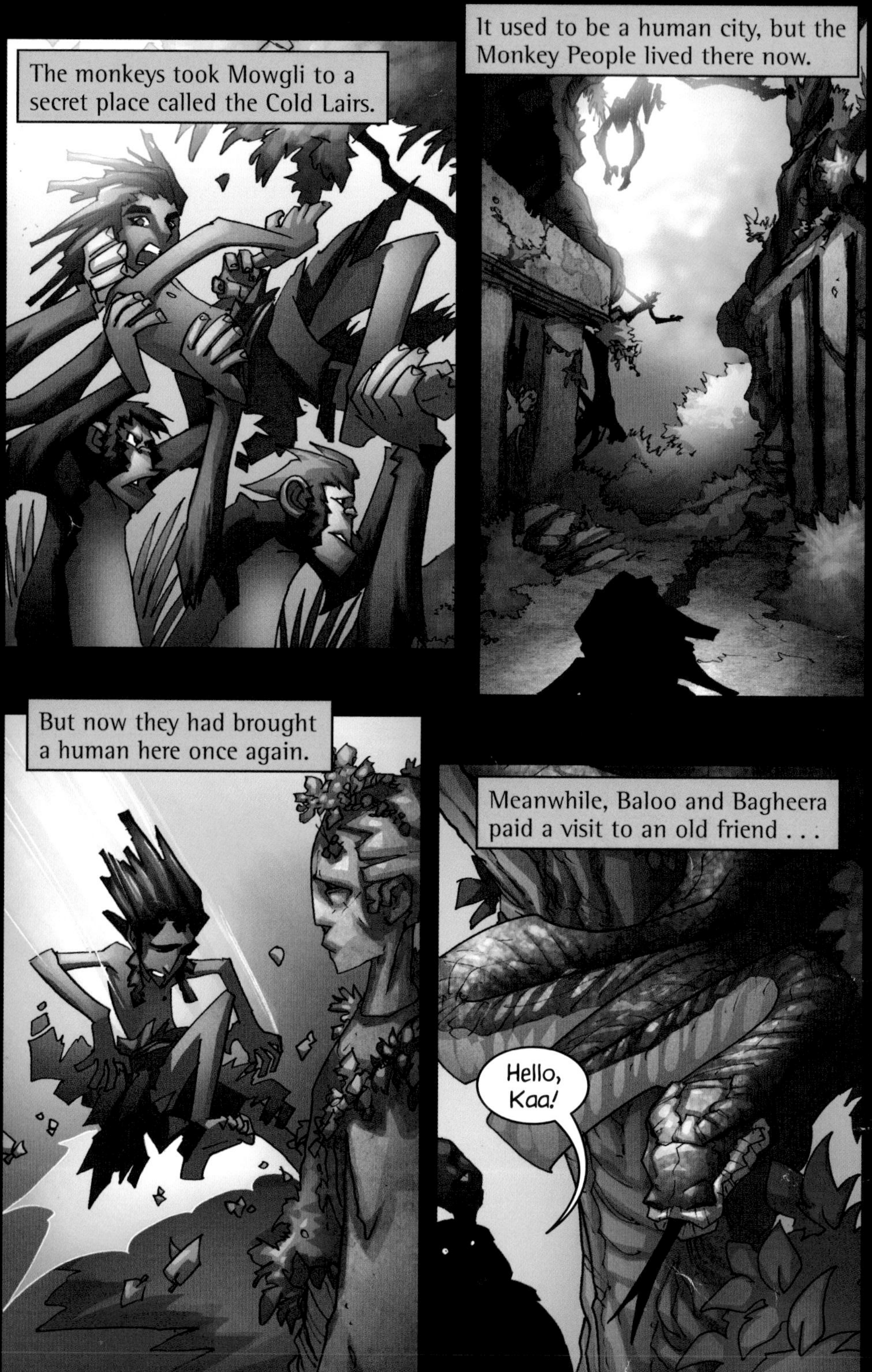

The monkeys took Mowgli to a secret place called the Cold Lairs.
It used to be a human city, but the Monkey People lived there now.
But now they had brought a human here once again.
Meanwhile, Baloo and Bagheera paid a visit to an old friend . . .
Hello, Kaa!

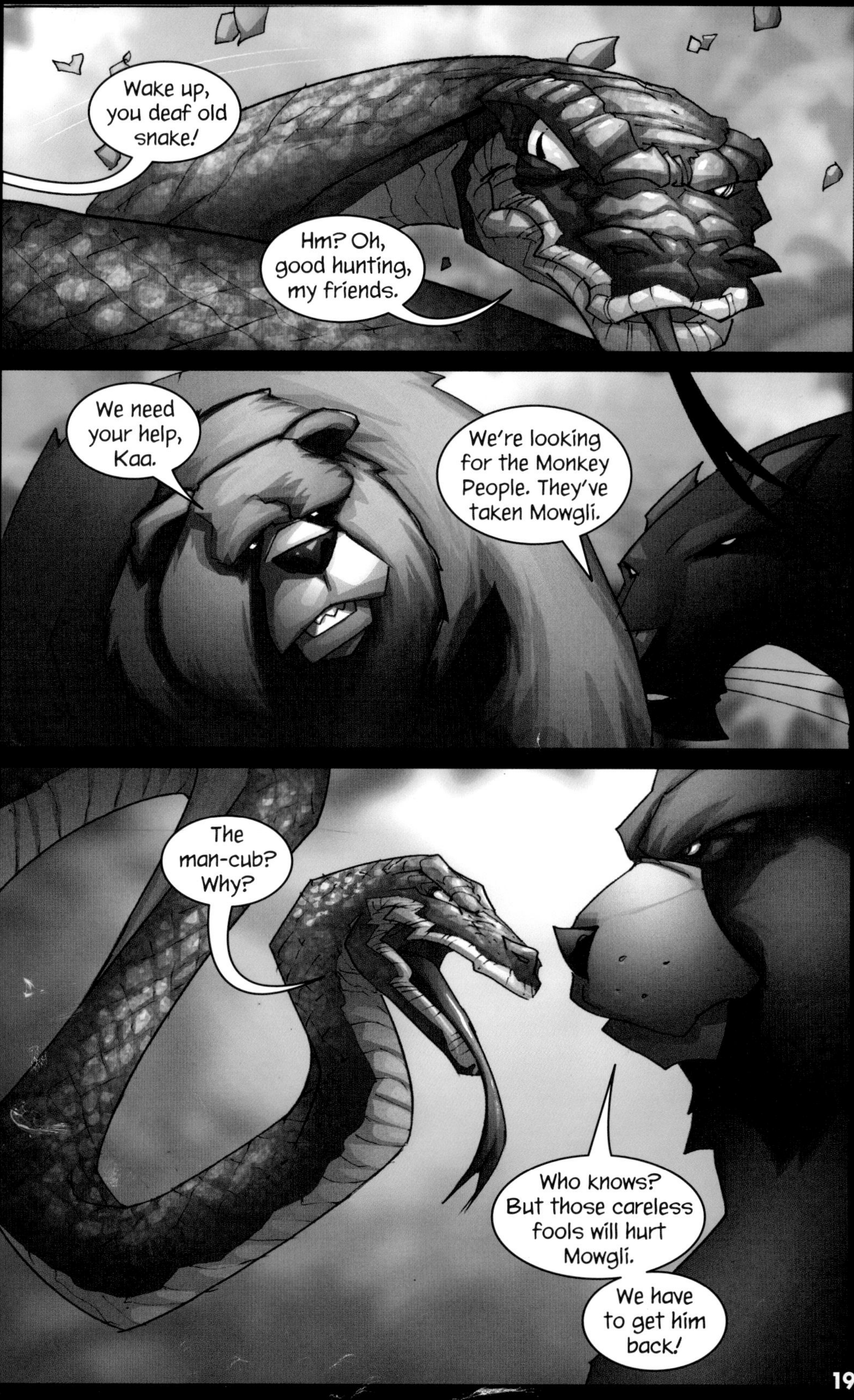
Wake up, you deaf old snake!
Hm? Oh, good hunting, my friends.
We need your help, Kaa.
We're looking for the Monkey People. They've taken Mowgli.
The man-cub? Why?
Who knows? But those careless fools will hurt Mowgli.
We have to get him back!

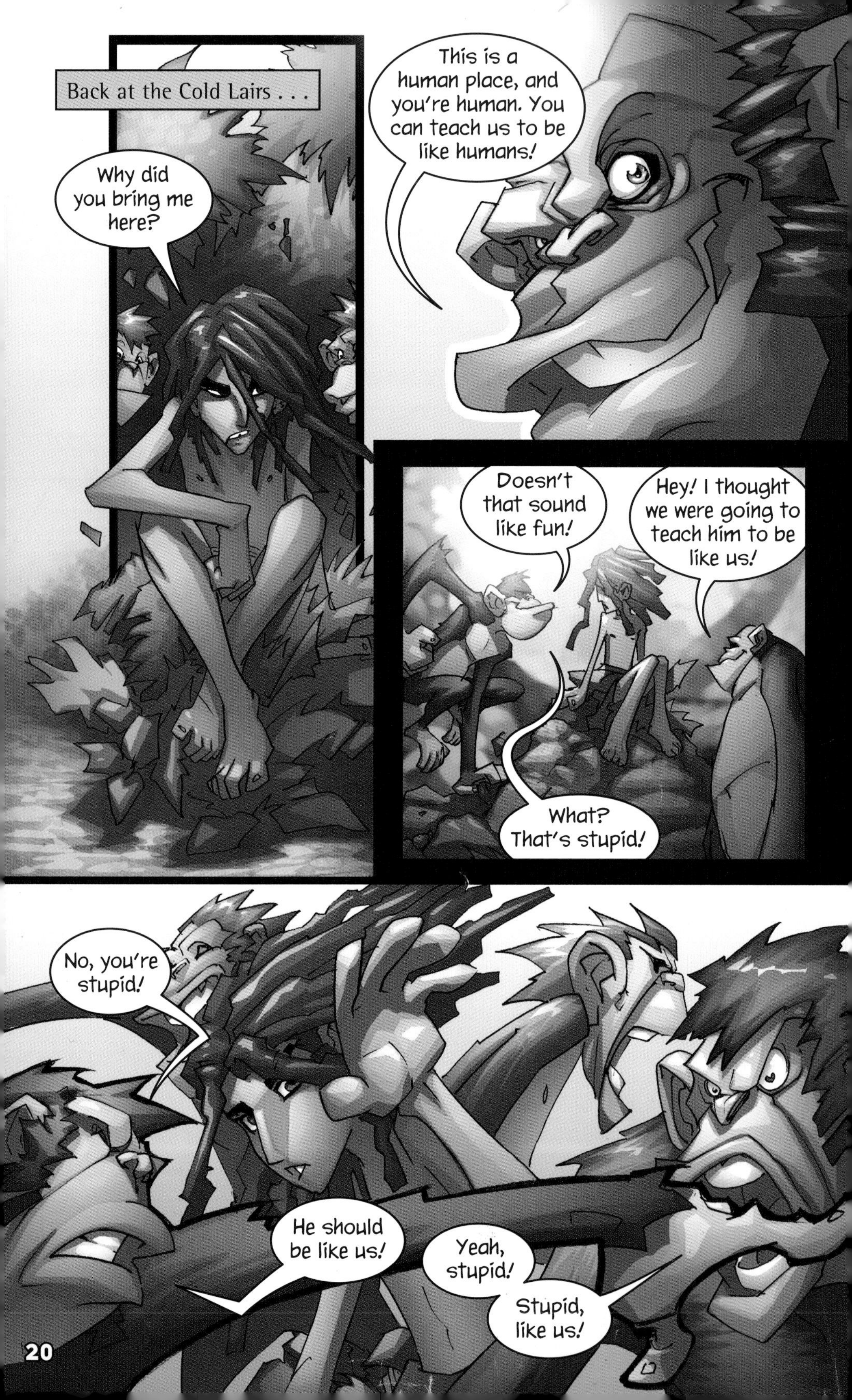

Back at the Cold Lairs . . .
Why did you bring me here?
This is a human place, and you're human. You can teach us to be like humans!
Doesn't that sound like fun!
Hey! I thought we were going to teach him to be like us!
What? That's stupid!
No, you're stupid!
He should be like us!
Yeah, stupid!
Stupid, like us!

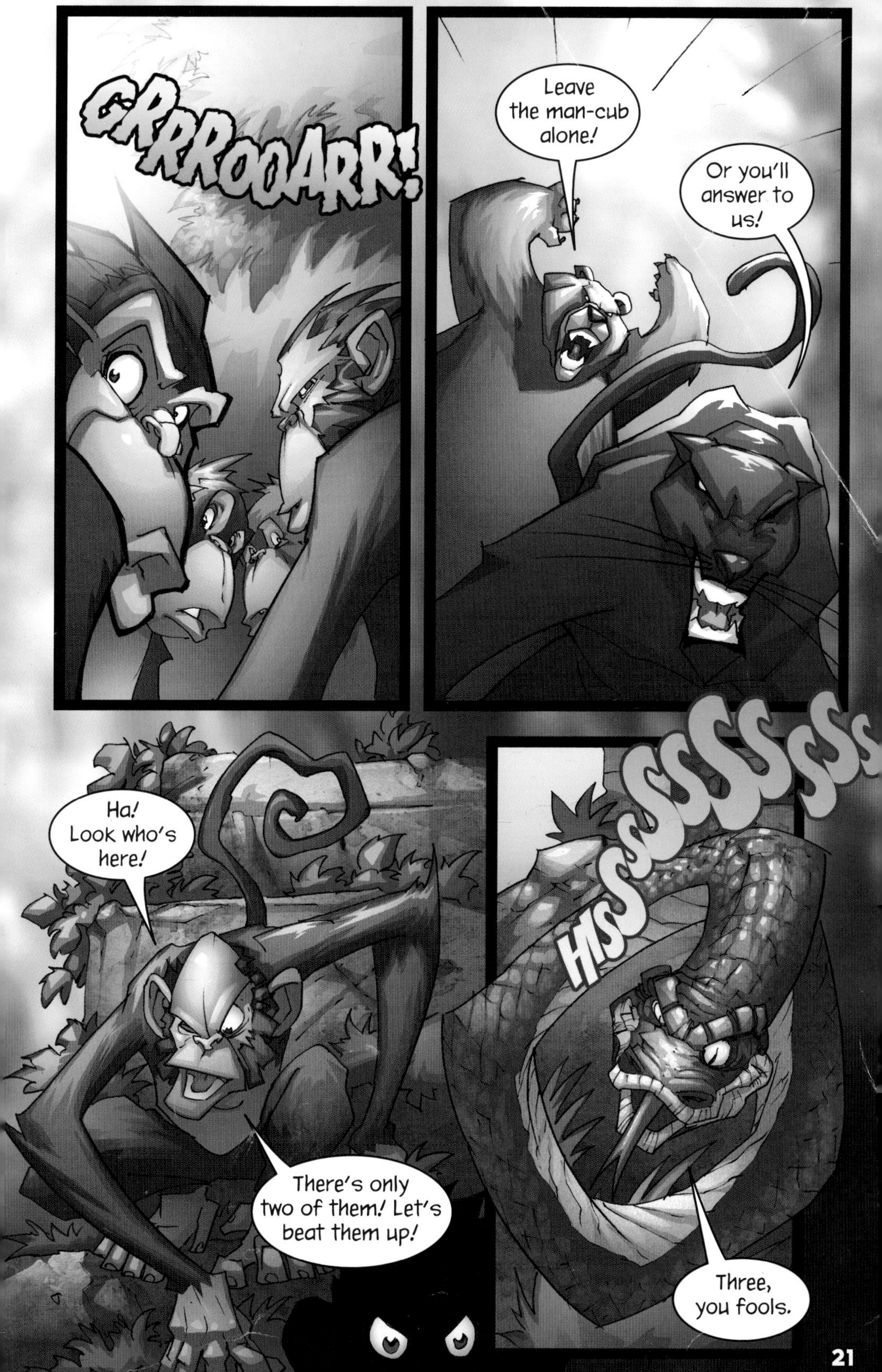
GRRROOARR!
Leave the man-cub alone!
Or you'll answer to us!
Ha! Look who's here!
There's only two of them! Let's beat them up!
HISSSSSSSSSSS
Three, you fools.

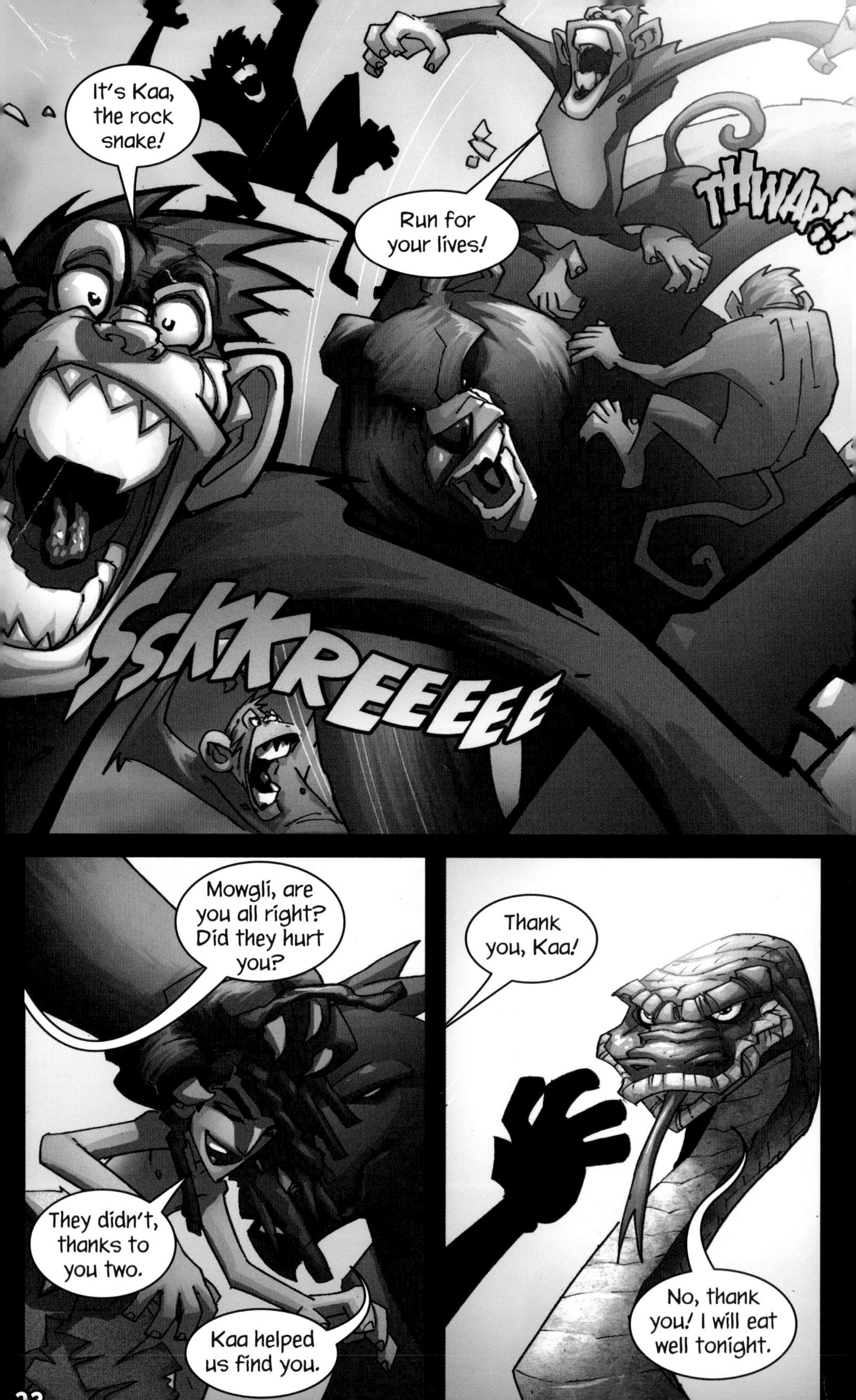
It's Kaa, the rock snake!
Run for your lives!
THWAP!!
SSKKREEEEEE
Mowgli, are you all right? Did they hurt you?
They didn't, thanks to you two.
Kaa helped us find you.
Thank you, Kaa!
No, thank you! I will eat well tonight.

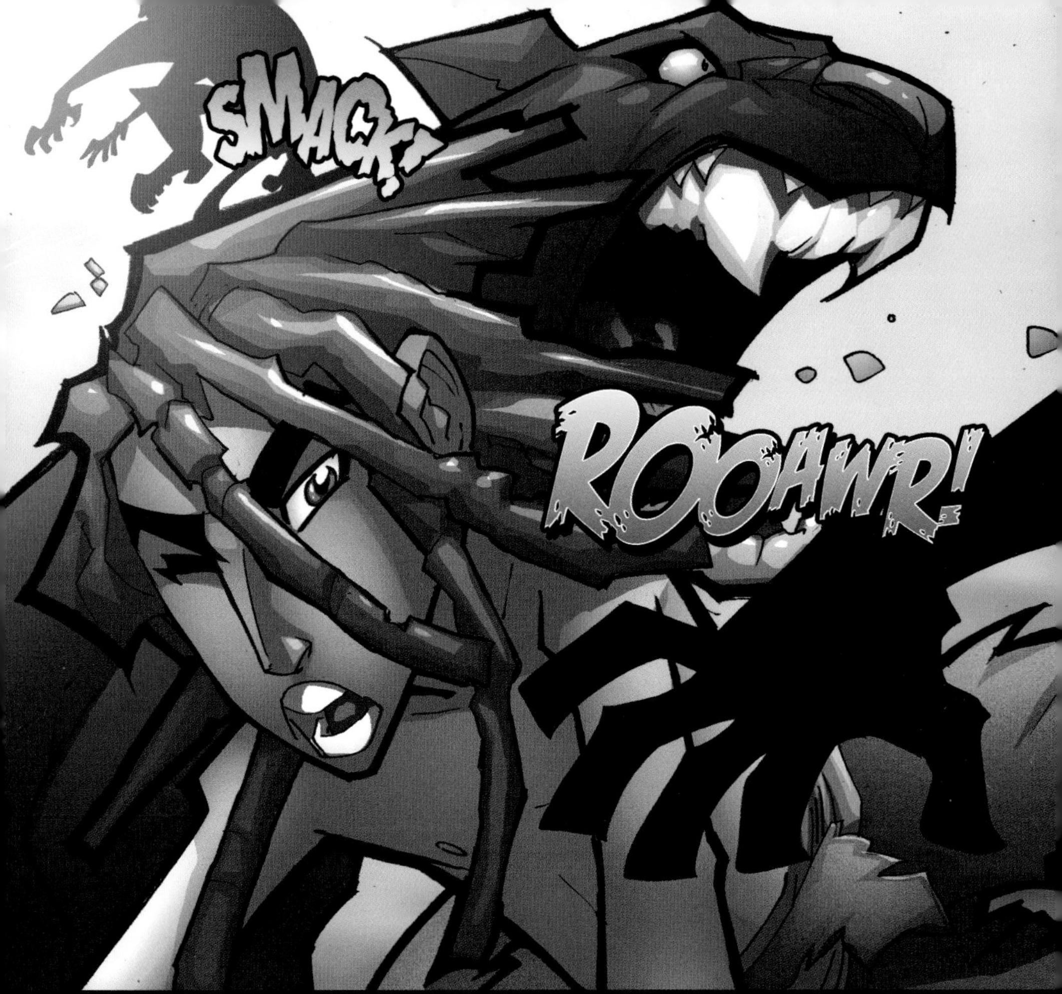
SMACK!
ROOAWR!

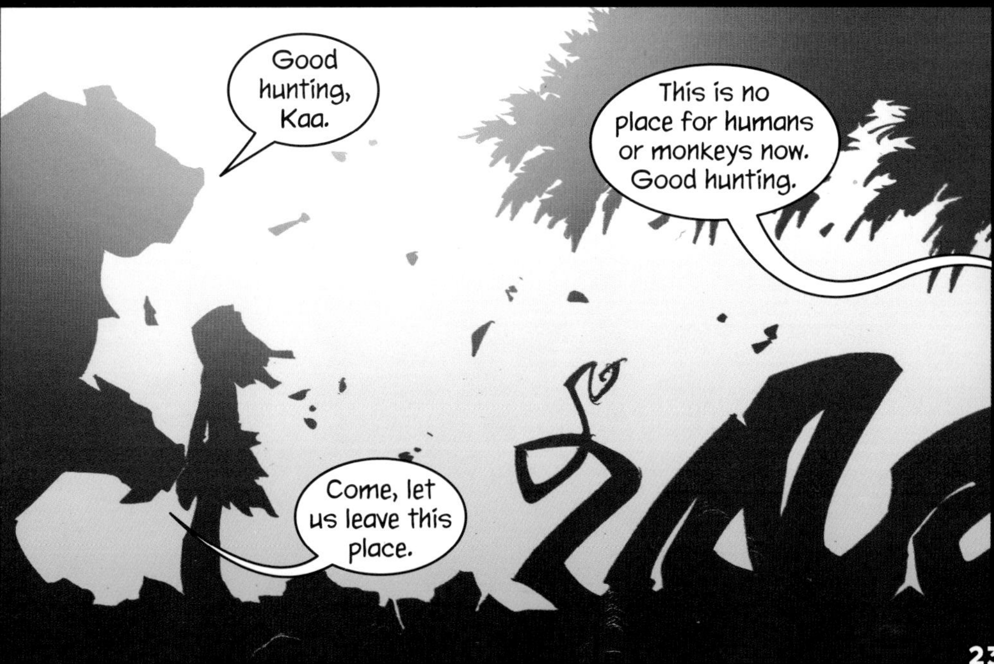
Good hunting, Kaa.
This is no place for humans or monkeys now. Good hunting.
Come, let us leave this place.

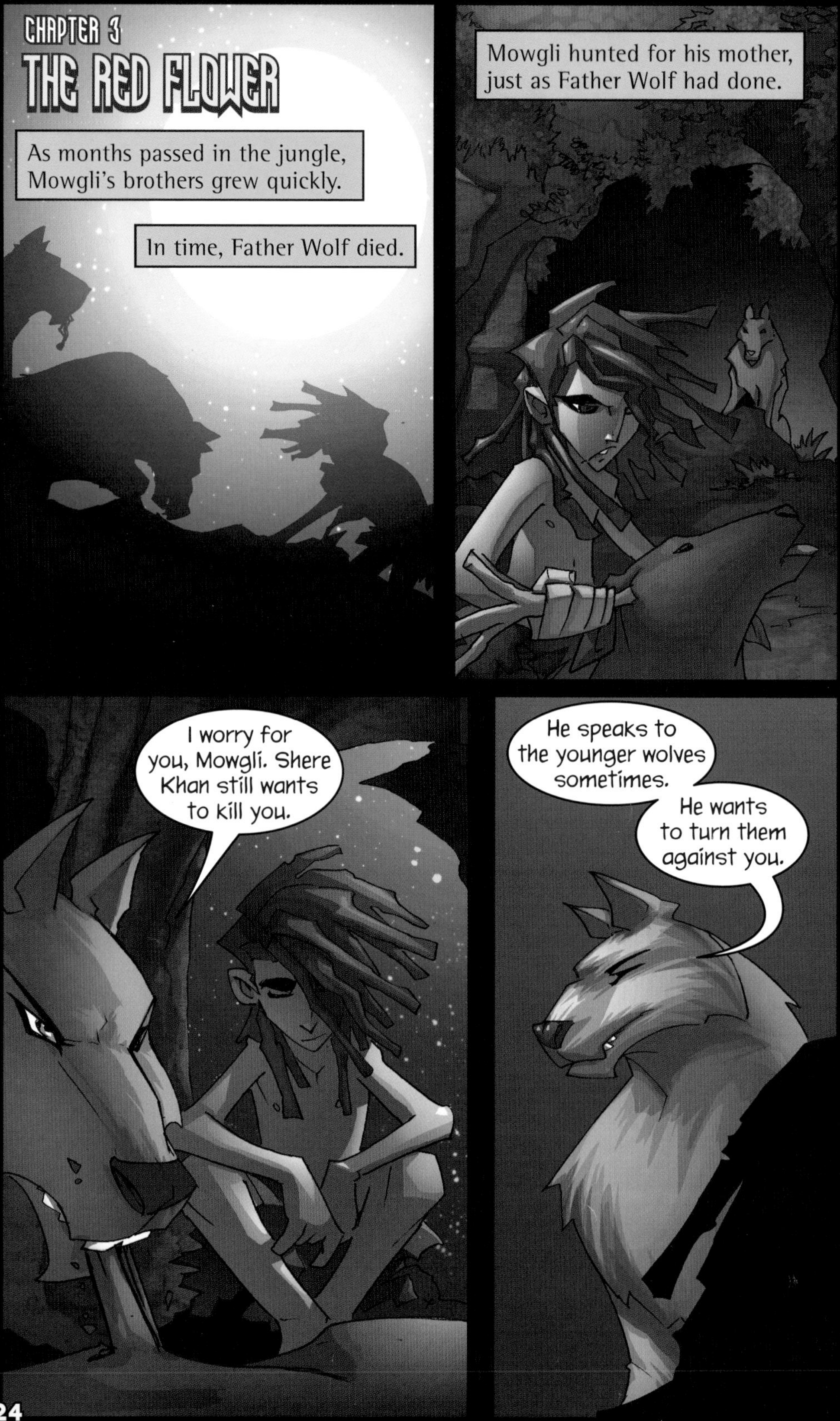
CHAPTER 3
THE RED FLOWER
As months passed in the jungle, Mowgli's brothers grew quickly.
In time, Father Wolf died.
Mowgli hunted for his mother, just as Father Wolf had done.
I worry for you, Mowgli. Shere Khan still wants to kill you.
He speaks to the younger wolves sometimes.
He wants to turn them against you.

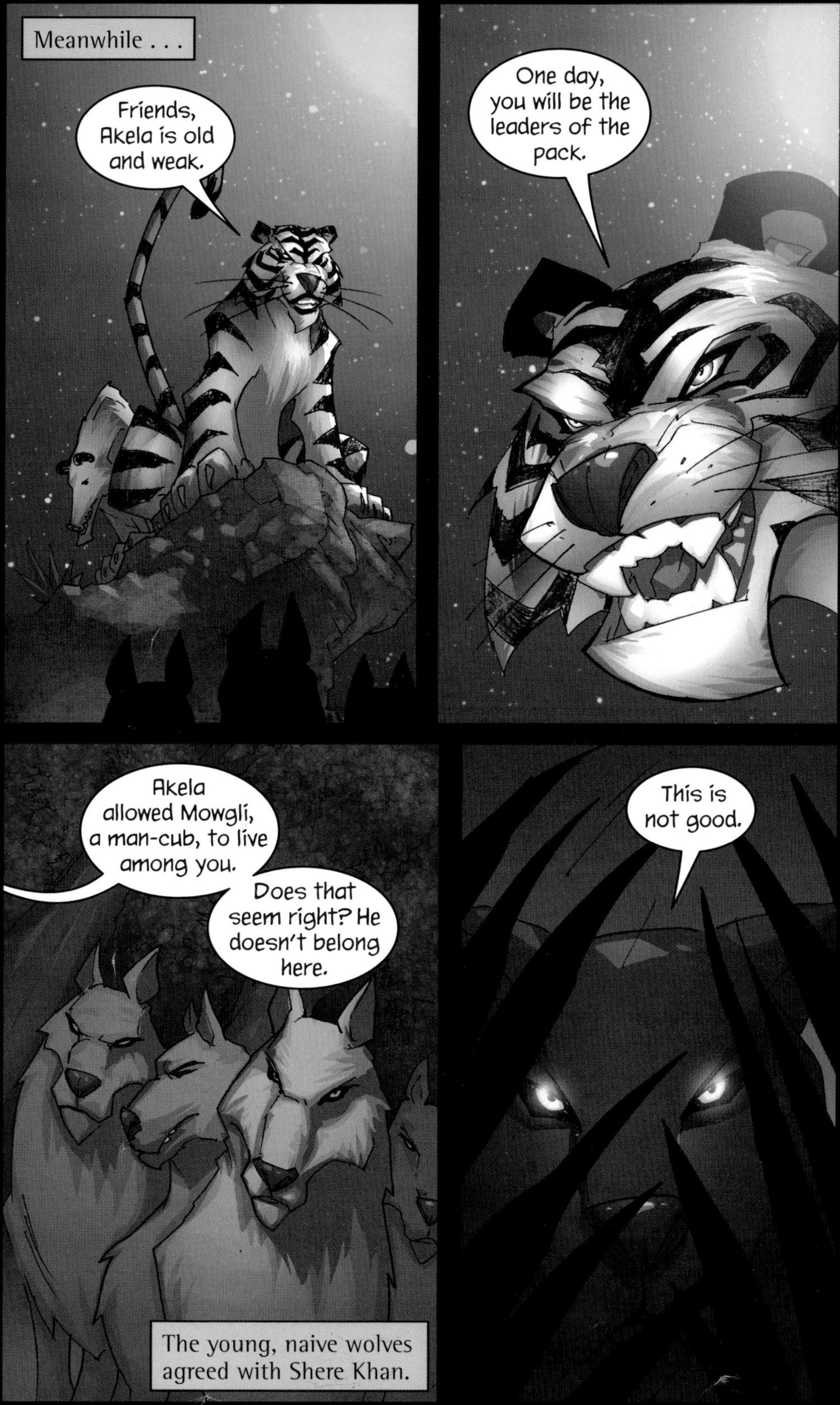
Meanwhile . . .
Friends, Akela is old and weak.
One day, you will be the leaders of the pack.
Akela allowed Mowgli, a man-cub, to live among you.
Does that seem right? He doesn't belong here.
The young, naive wolves agreed with Shere Khan.
This is not good.

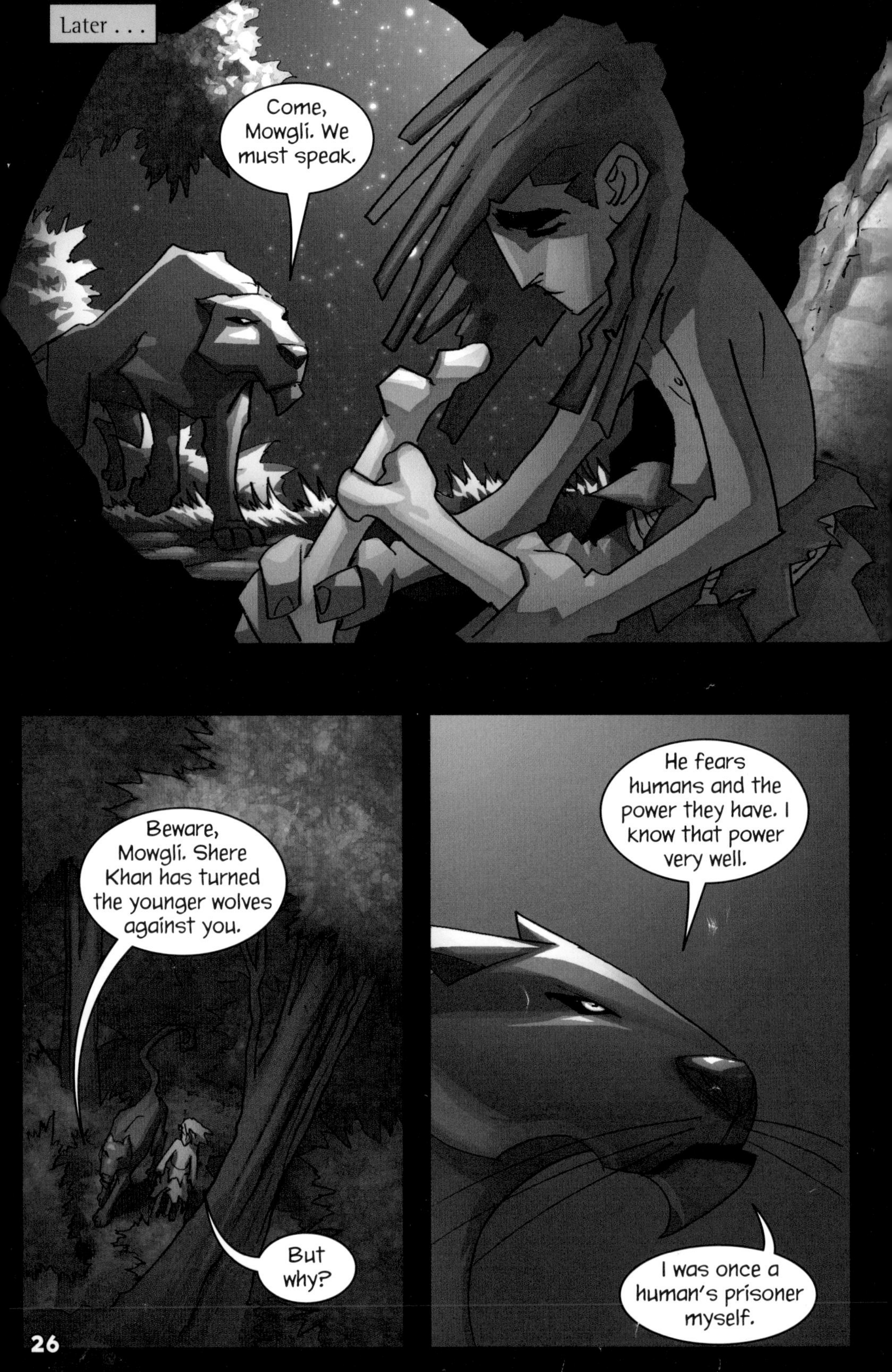
Later . . .
Come, Mowgli. We must speak.
Beware, Mowgli. Shere Khan has turned the younger wolves against you.
But why?
He fears humans and the power they have. I know that power very well.
I was once a human's prisoner myself.

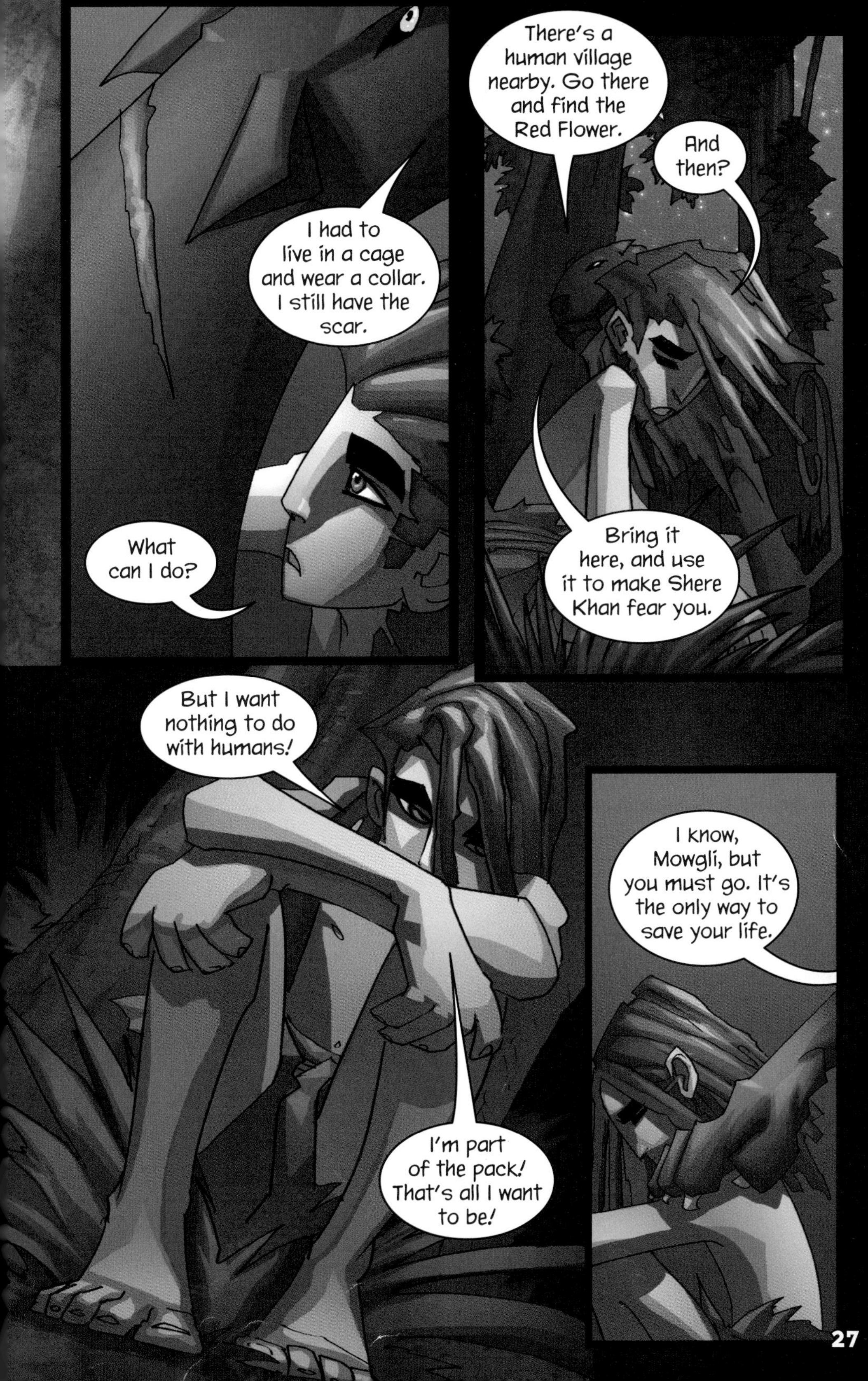
I had to live in a cage and wear a collar. I still have the scar.
What can I do?
There's a human village nearby. Go there and find the Red Flower.
And then?
Bring it here, and use it to make Shere Khan fear you.
But I want nothing to do with humans!
I'm part of the pack! That's all I want to be!
I know, Mowgli, but you must go. It's the only way to save your life.

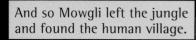
And so Mowgli left the jungle and found the human village.

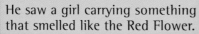
He saw a girl carrying something that smelled like the Red Flower.

Frightened by Mowgli, the girl dropped what she was carrying and ran away.

Within, Mowgli found a seed of the Red Flower.

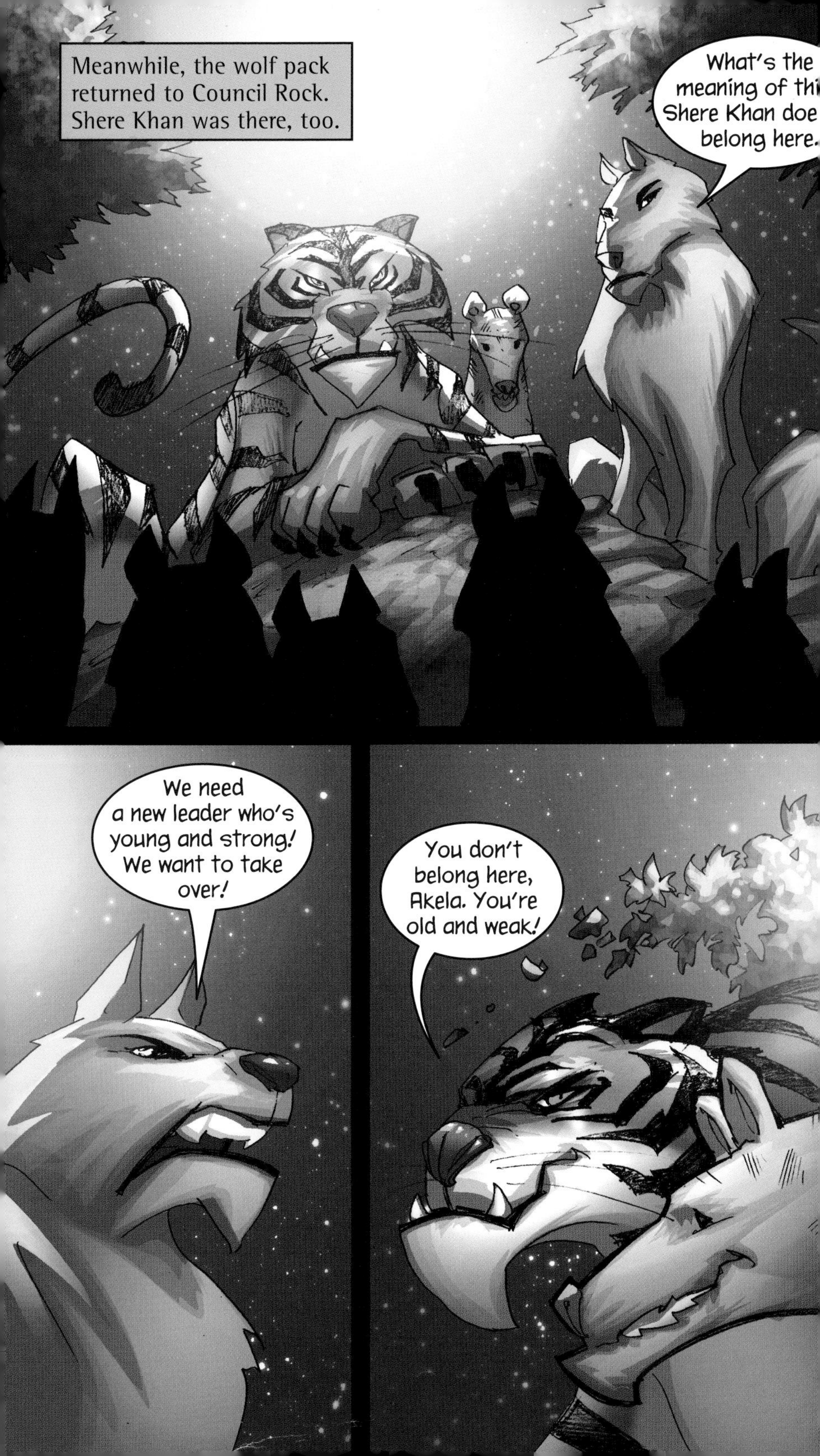
Meanwhile, the wolf pack returned to Council Rock. Shere Khan was there, too.
What's the meaning of thi Shere Khan doe belong here.
We need a new leader who's young and strong! We want to take over!
You don't belong here, Akela. You're old and weak!

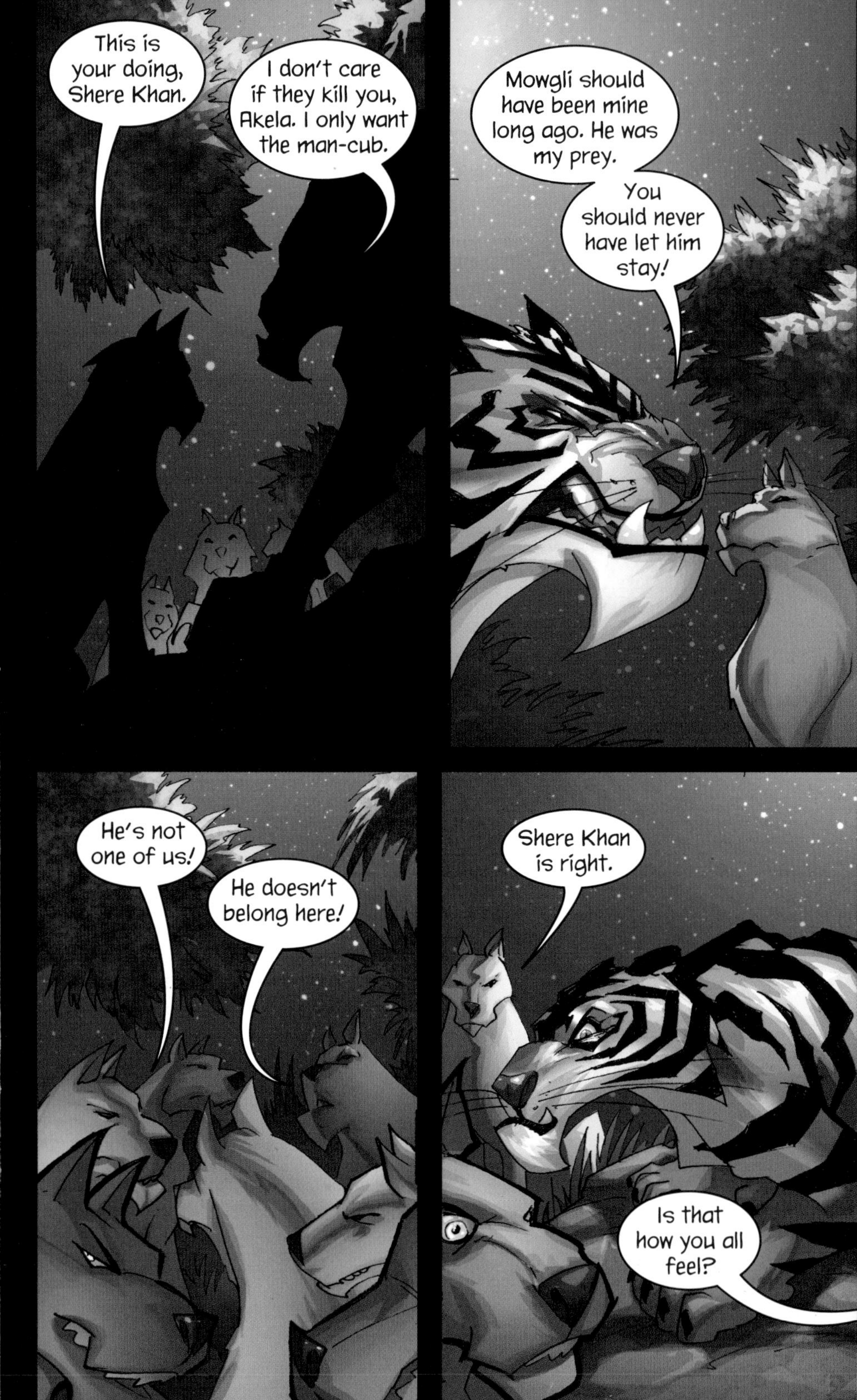
This is your doing, Shere Khan.
I don't care if they kill you, Akela. I only want the man-cub.
Mowgli should have been mine long ago. He was my prey.
You should never have let him stay!
He's not one of us!
He doesn't belong here!
Shere Khan is right.
Is that how you all feel?

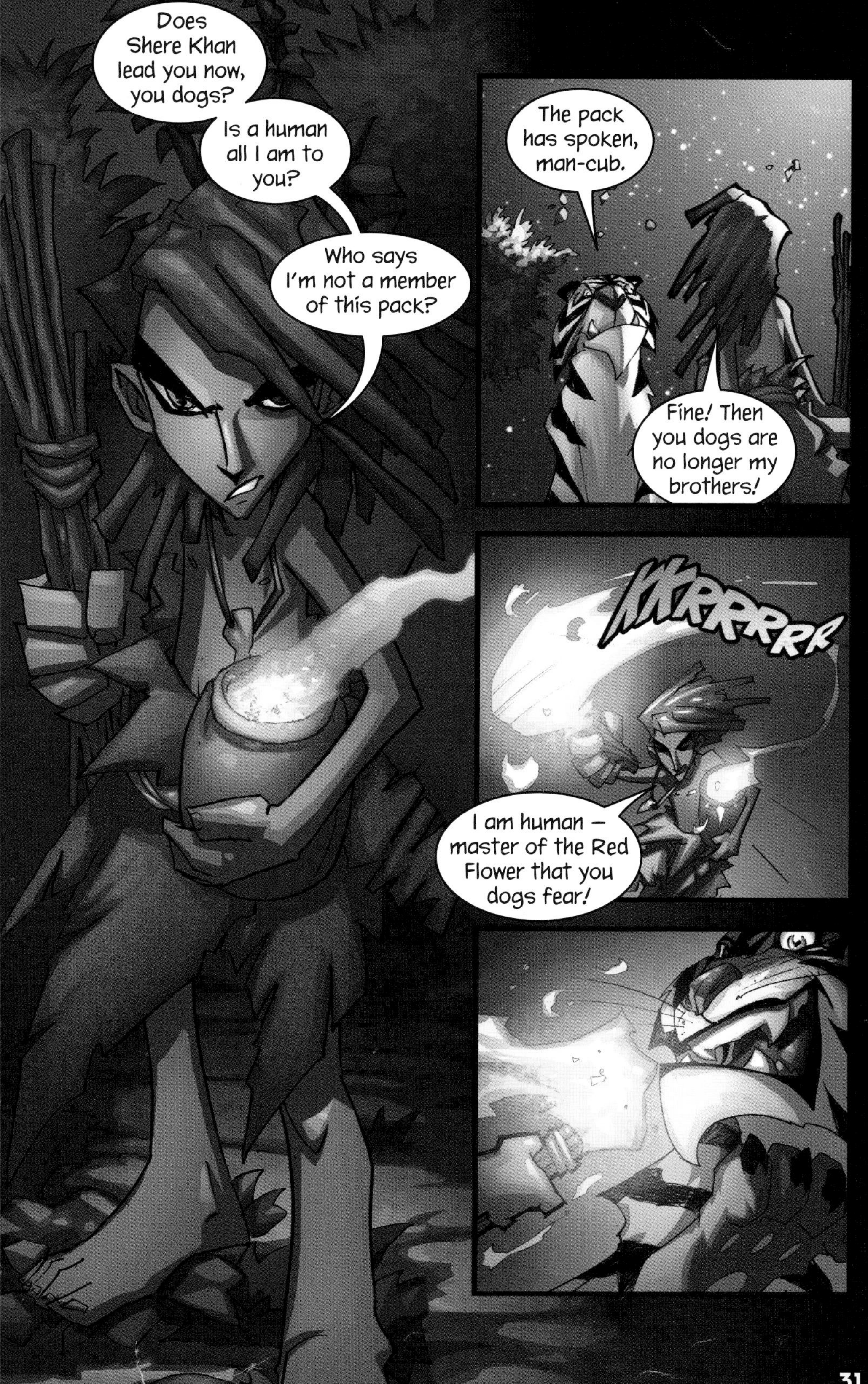
Does Shere Khan lead you now, you dogs?
Is a human all I am to you?
Who says I'm not a member of this pack?
The pack has spoken, man-cub.
Fine! Then you dogs are no longer my brothers!
KKRRRRRR
I am human — master of the Red Flower that you dogs fear!

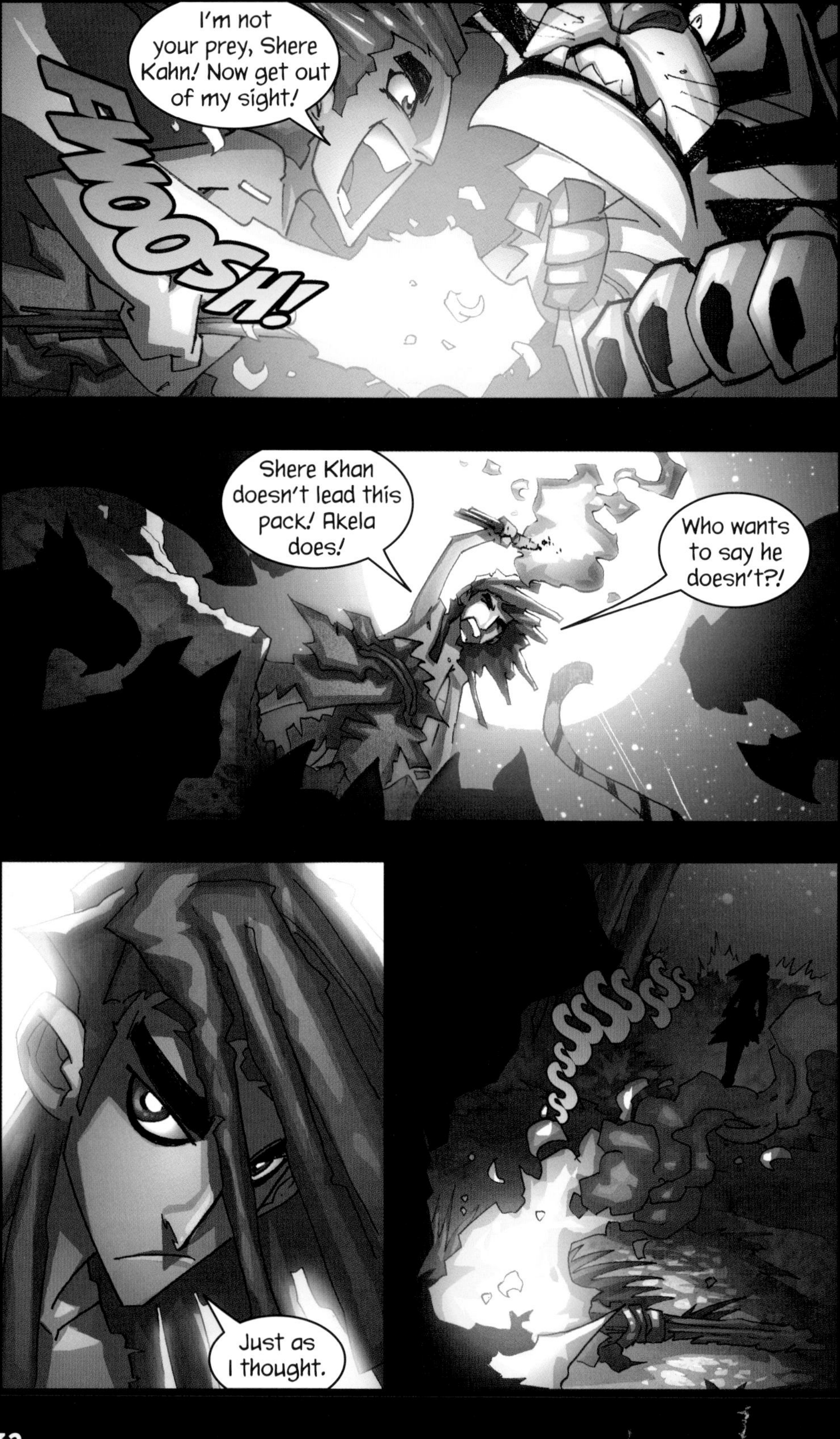
I'm not your prey, Shere Kahn! Now get out of my sight!
FWOOSH!
Shere Khan doesn't lead this pack! Akela does!
Who wants to say he doesn't?!
Just as I thought.

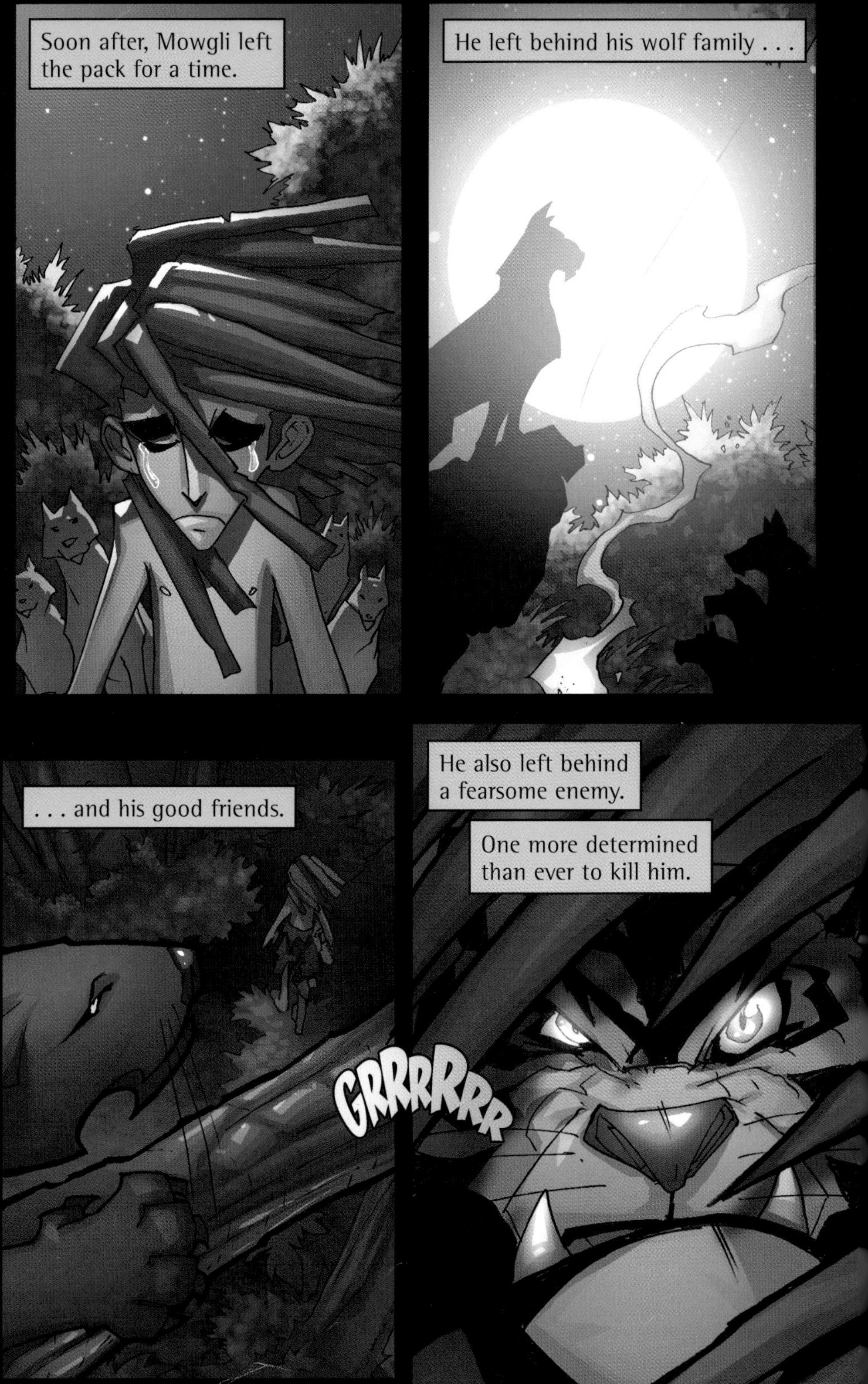
Soon after, Mowgli left the pack for a time.
He left behind his wolf family . . .
. . . and his good friends.
He also left behind a fearsome enemy.
One more determined than ever to kill him.
GRRRRRR

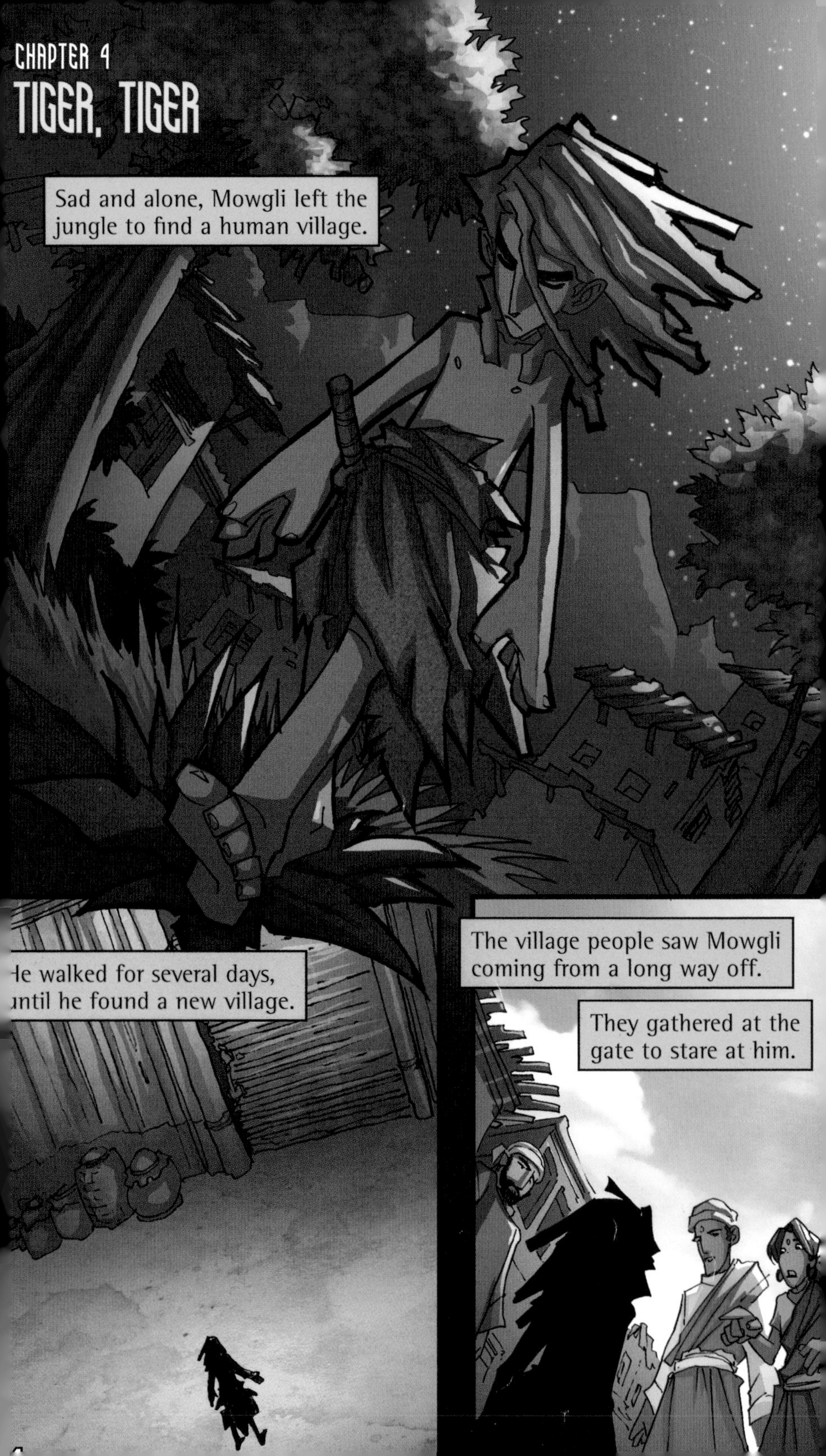
CHAPTER 4
TIGER, TIGER
Sad and alone, Mowgli left the jungle to find a human village.
He walked for several days, until he found a new village.
The village people saw Mowgli coming from a long way off.
They gathered at the gate to stare at him.

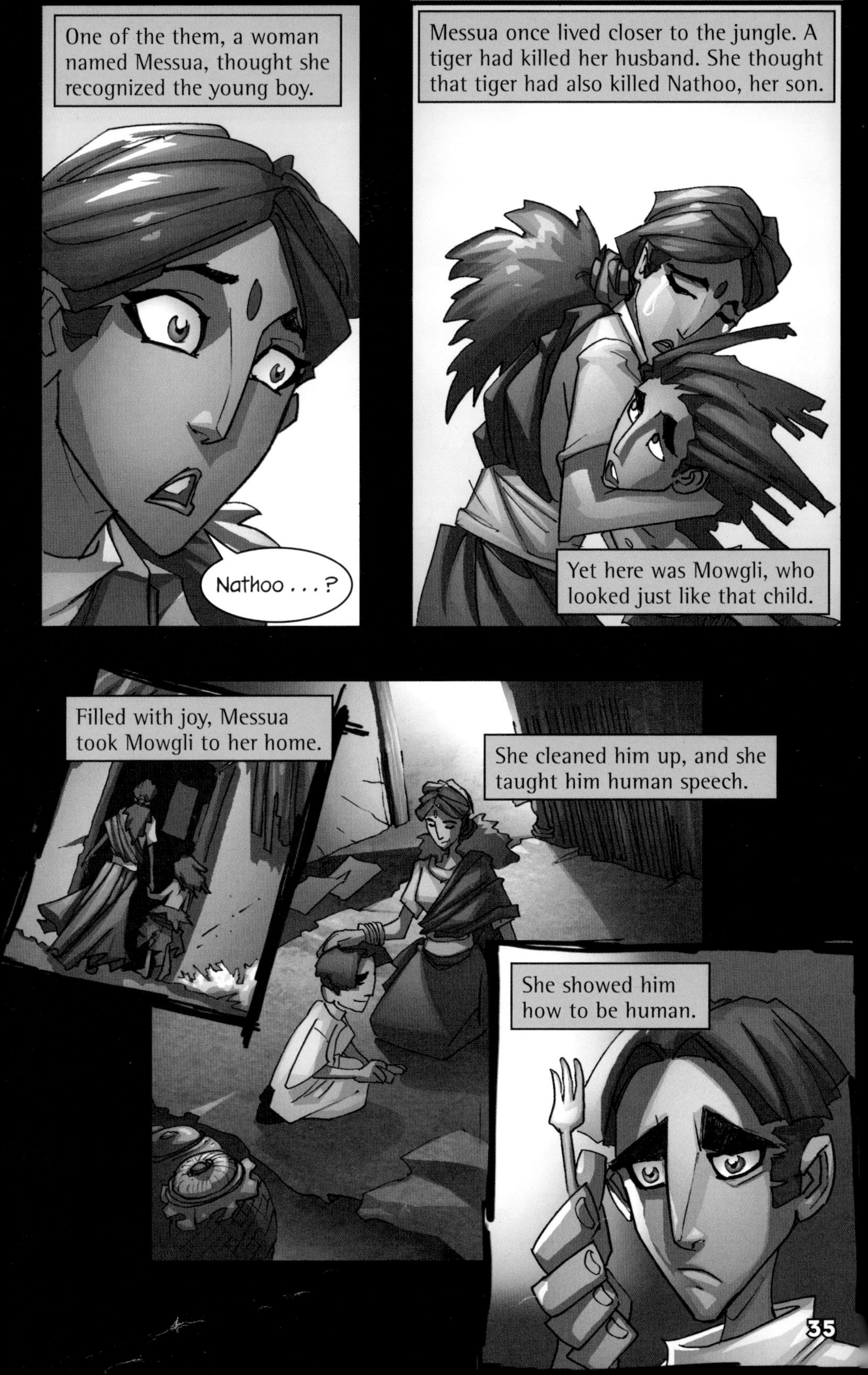
One of the them, a woman named Messua, thought she recognized the young boy.
Nathoo . . . ?
Messua once lived closer to the jungle. A tiger had killed her husband. She thought that tiger had also killed Nathoo, her son.
Yet here was Mowgli, who looked just like that child.
Filled with joy, Messua took Mowgli to her home.
She cleaned him up, and she taught him human speech.
She showed him how to be human.

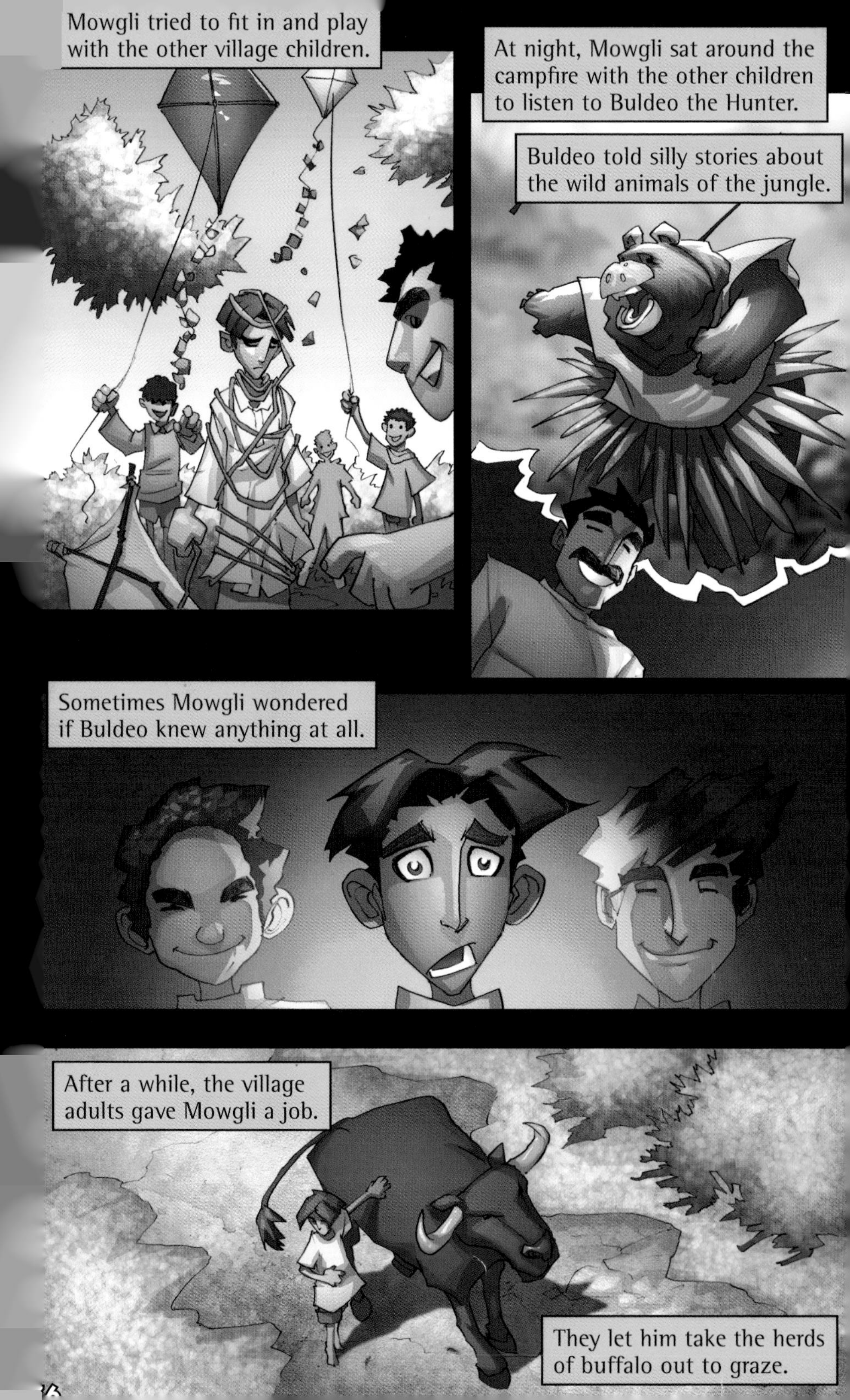
Mowgli tried to fit in and play with the other village children.
At night, Mowgli sat around the campfire with the other children to listen to Buldeo the Hunter.
Buldeo told silly stories about the wild animals of the jungle.
Sometimes Mowgli wondered if Buldeo knew anything at all.
After a while, the village adults gave Mowgli a job.
They let him take the herds of buffalo out to graze.

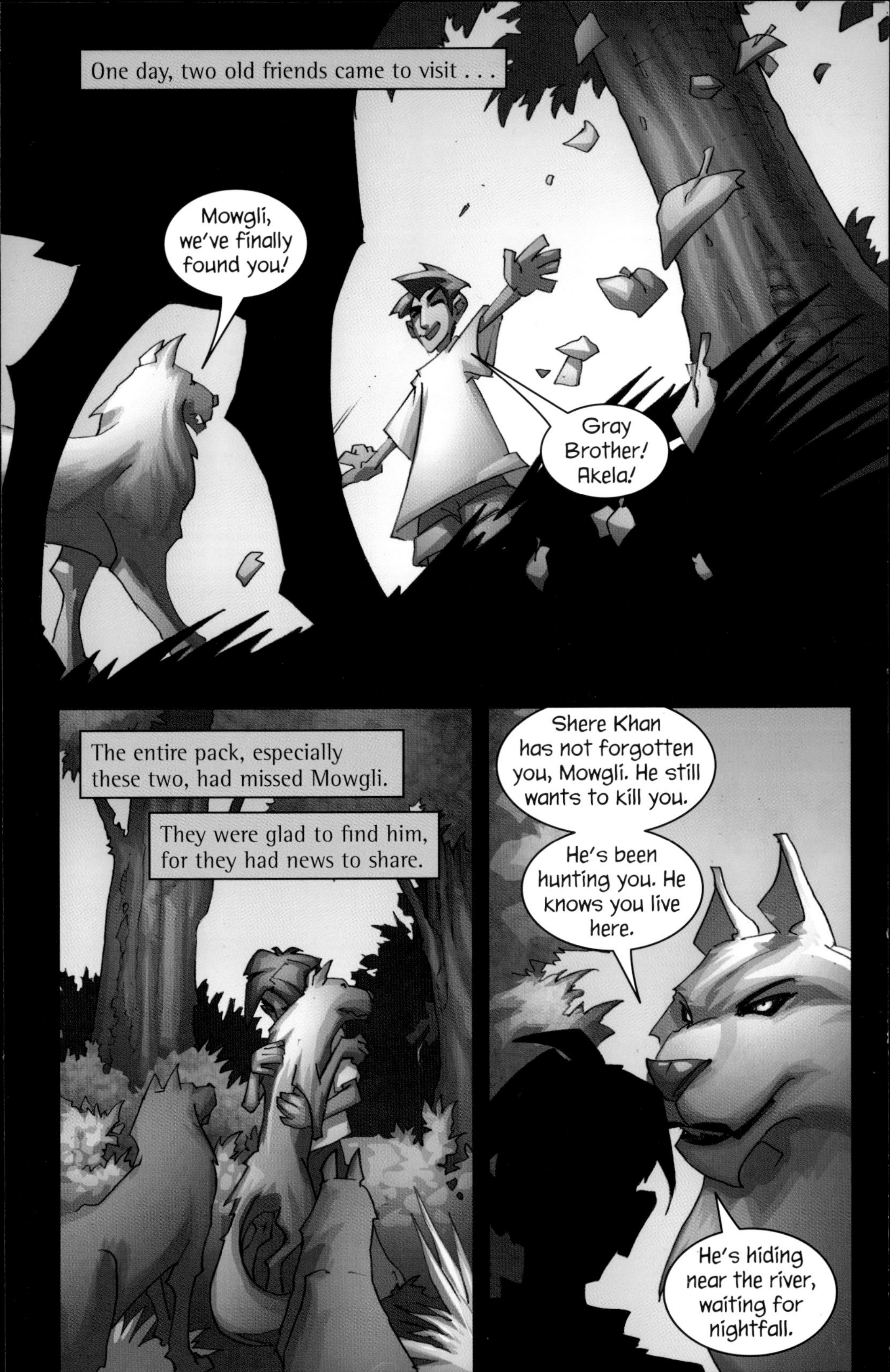
One day, two old friends came to visit . . .
Mowgli, we've finally found you!
Gray Brother! Akela!
The entire pack, especially these two, had missed Mowgli.
They were glad to find him, for they had news to share.
Shere Khan has not forgotten you, Mowgli. He still wants to kill you.
He's been hunting you. He knows you live here.
He's hiding near the river, waiting for nightfall.

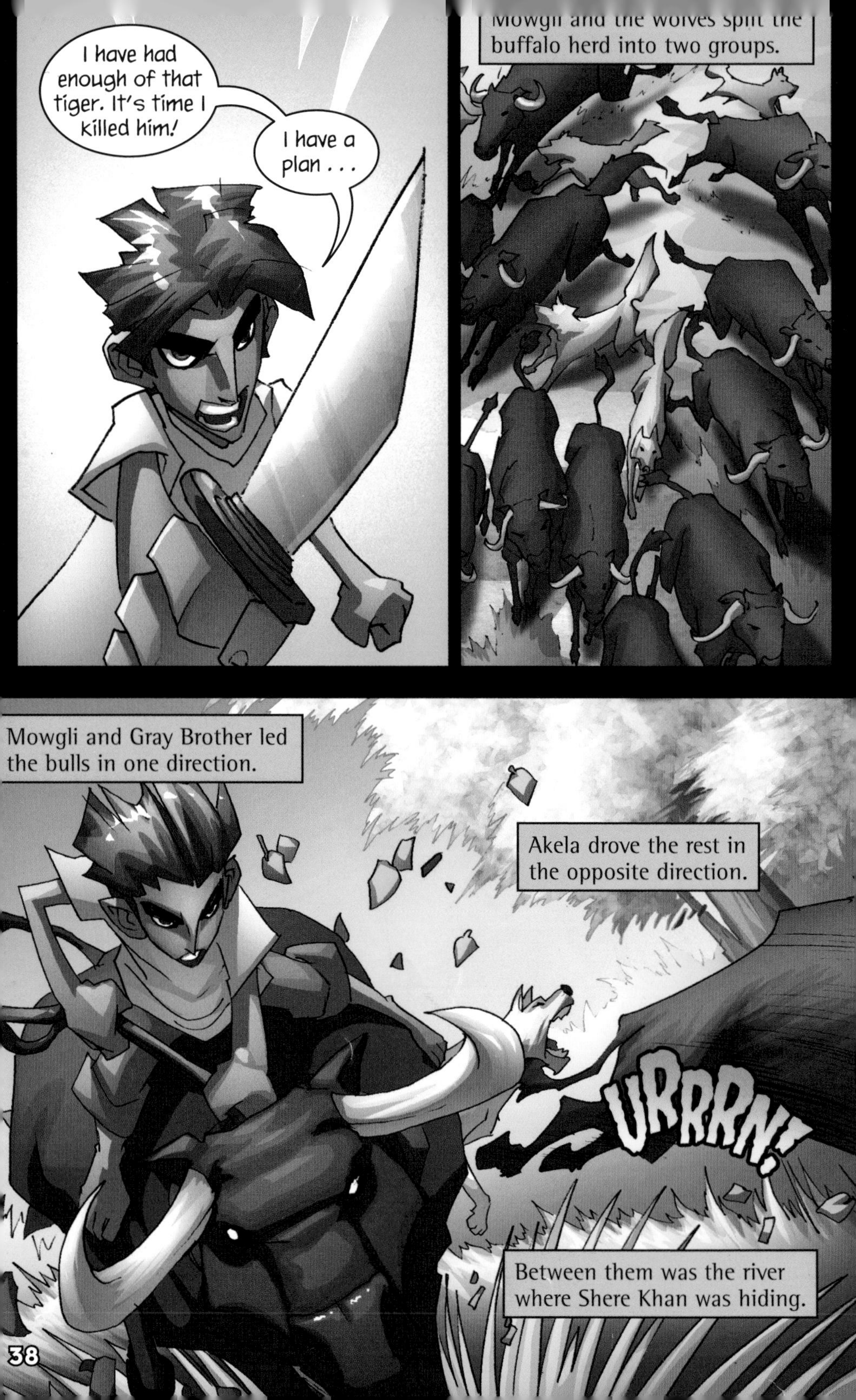
I have had enough of that tiger. It's time I killed him!
I have a plan . . .
Mowgli and the wolves split the buffalo herd into two groups.
Mowgli and Gray Brother led the bulls in one direction.
Akela drove the rest in the opposite direction.
URRRN!
Between them was the river where Shere Khan was hiding.

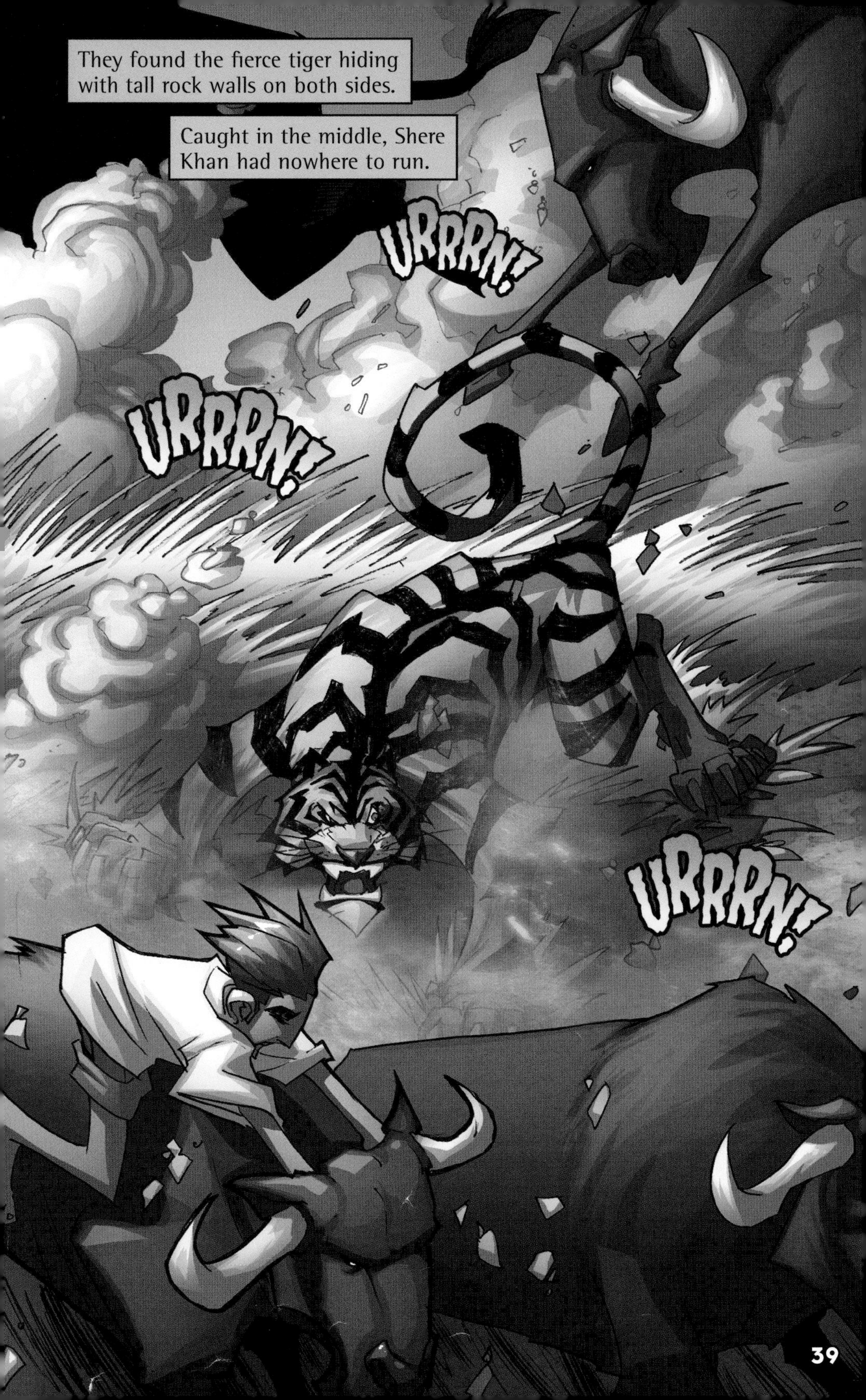
They found the fierce tiger hiding with tall rock walls on both sides.
Caught in the middle, Shere Khan had nowhere to run.
URRRN!
URRRN!
URRRN!

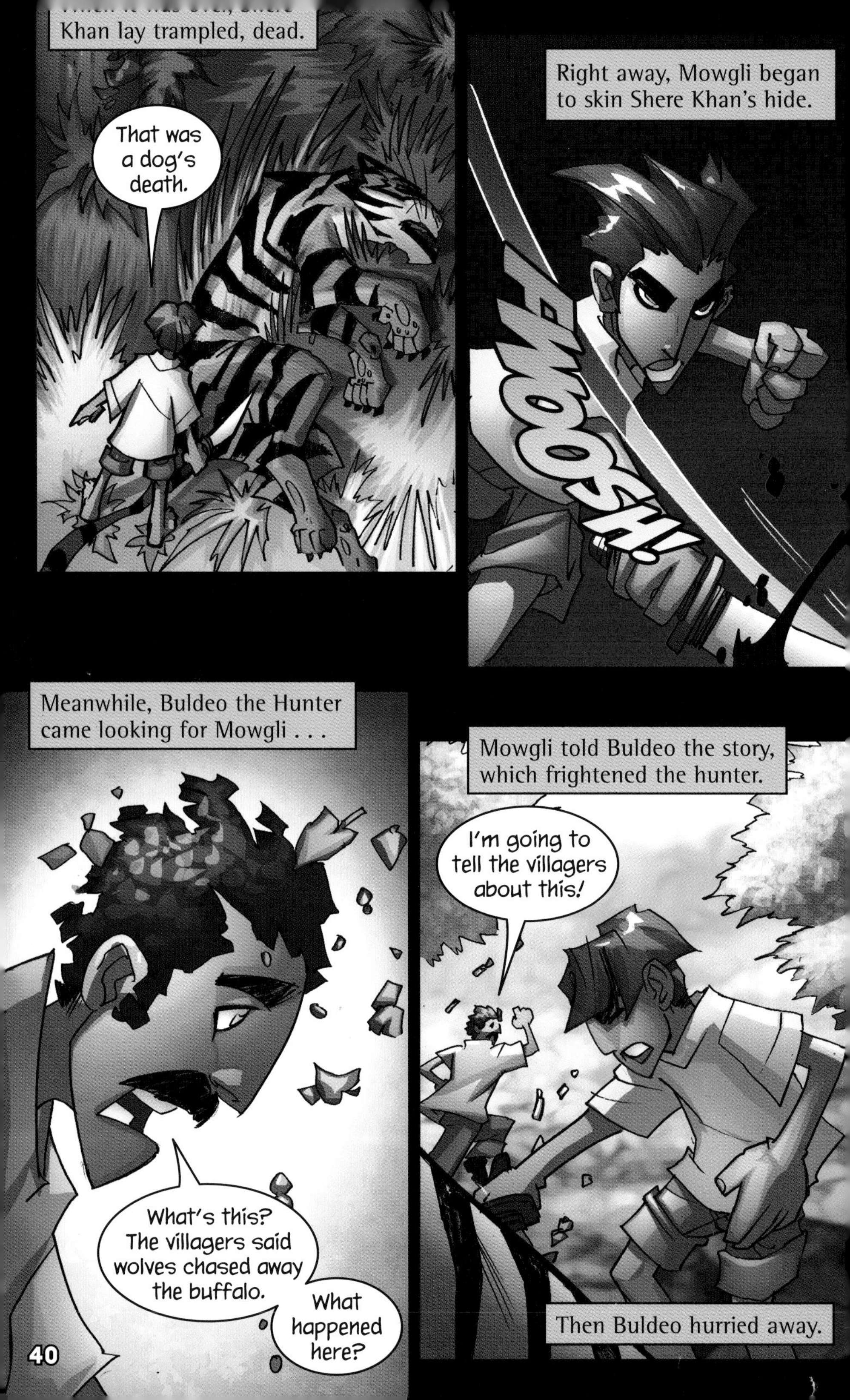
Khan lay trampled, dead.
That was a dog's death.
Right away, Mowgli began to skin Shere Khan's hide.
FWOOSH!
Meanwhile, Buldeo the Hunter came looking for Mowgli . . .
What's this? The villagers said wolves chased away the buffalo.
What happened here?
Mowgli told Buldeo the story, which frightened the hunter.
I'm going to tell the villagers about this!
Then Buldeo hurried away.

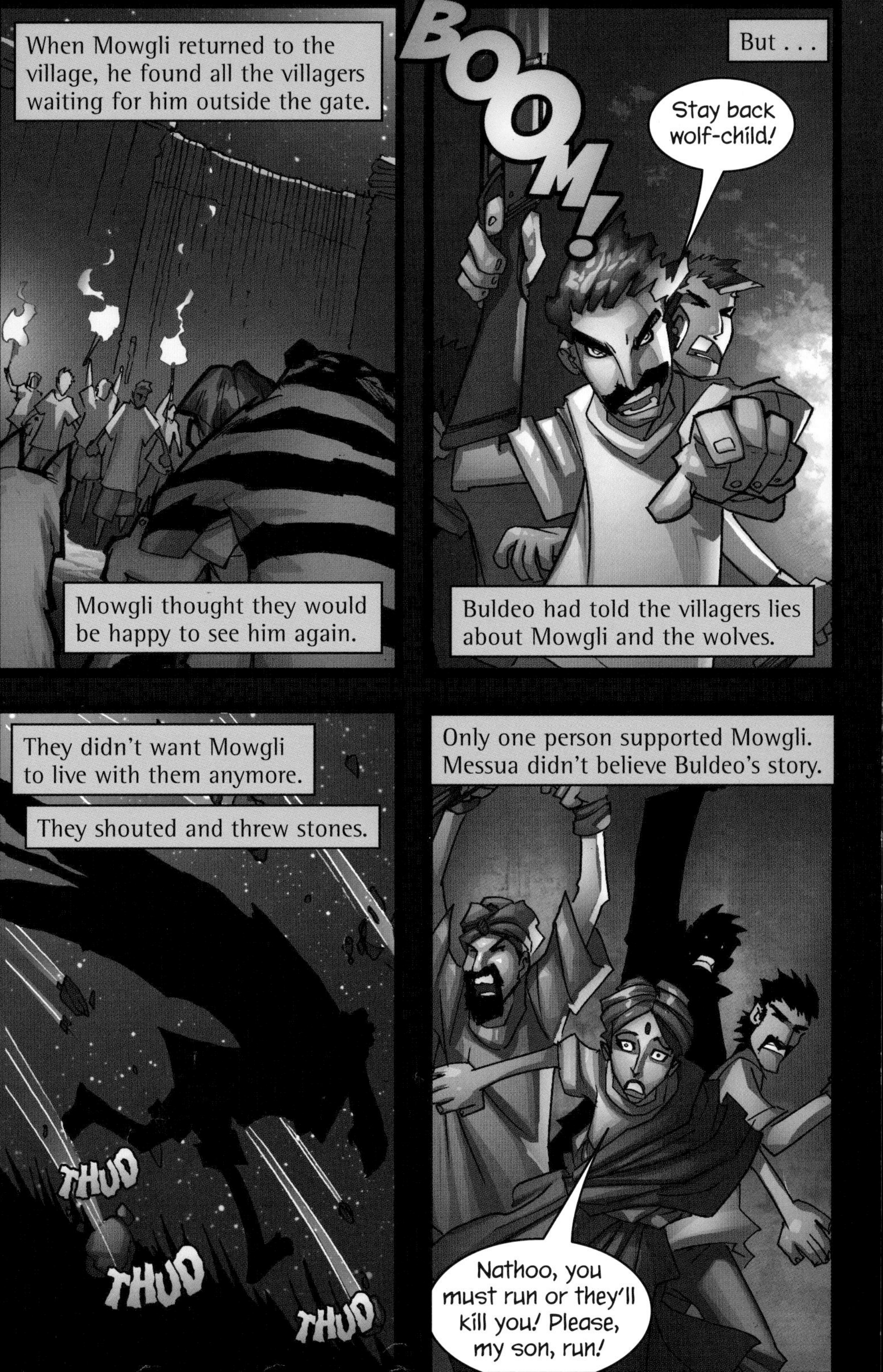
When Mowgli returned to the village, he found all the villagers waiting for him outside the gate.
Mowgli thought they would be happy to see him again.
BOOM!
But . . .
Stay back wolf-child!
Buldeo had told the villagers lies about Mowgli and the wolves.
They didn't want Mowgli to live with them anymore.
They shouted and threw stones.
THUD
THUD
THUD
Only one person supported Mowgli. Messua didn't believe Buldeo's story.
Nathoo, you must run or they'll kill you! Please, my son, run!

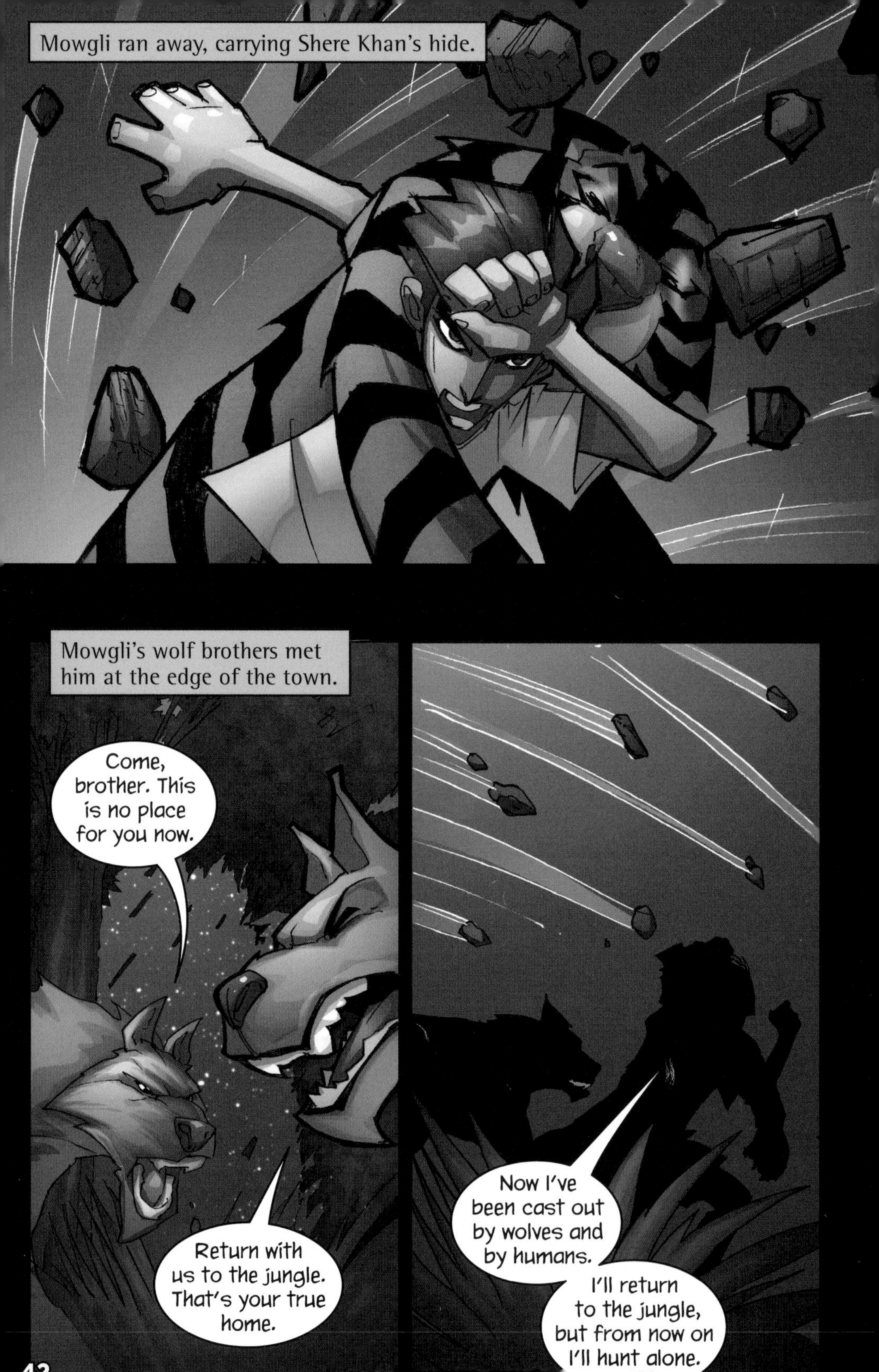
Mowgli ran away, carrying Shere Khan's hide.
Mowgli's wolf brothers met him at the edge of the town.
Come, brother. This is no place for you now.
Return with us to the jungle. That's your true home.
Now I've been cast out by wolves and by humans.
I'll return to the jungle, but from now on I'll hunt alone.

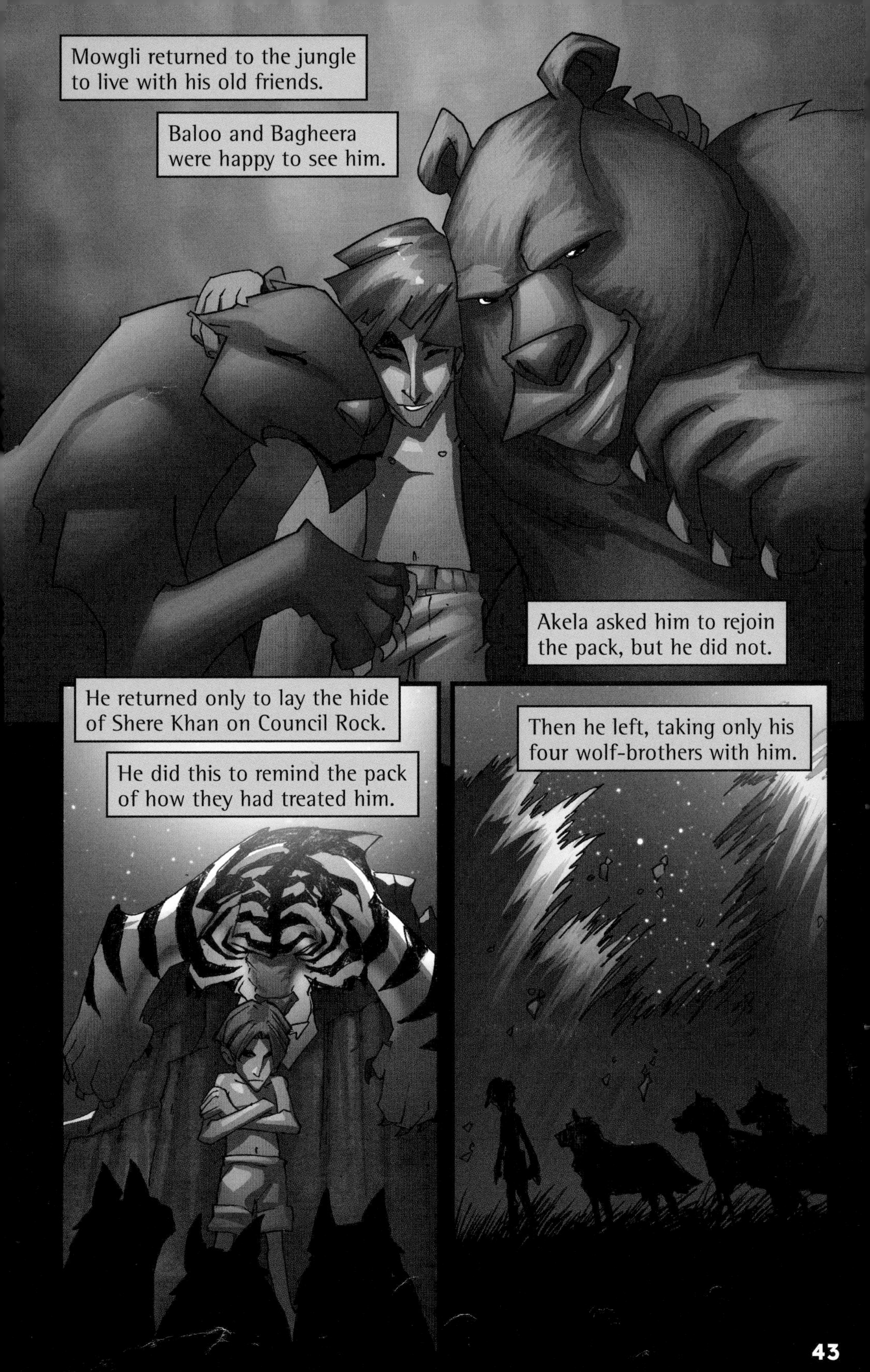
Mowgli returned to the jungle to live with his old friends.
Baloo and Bagheera were happy to see him.
Akela asked him to rejoin the pack, but he did not.
He returned only to lay the hide of Shere Khan on Council Rock.
He did this to remind the pack of how they had treated him.
Then he left, taking only his four wolf-brothers with him.

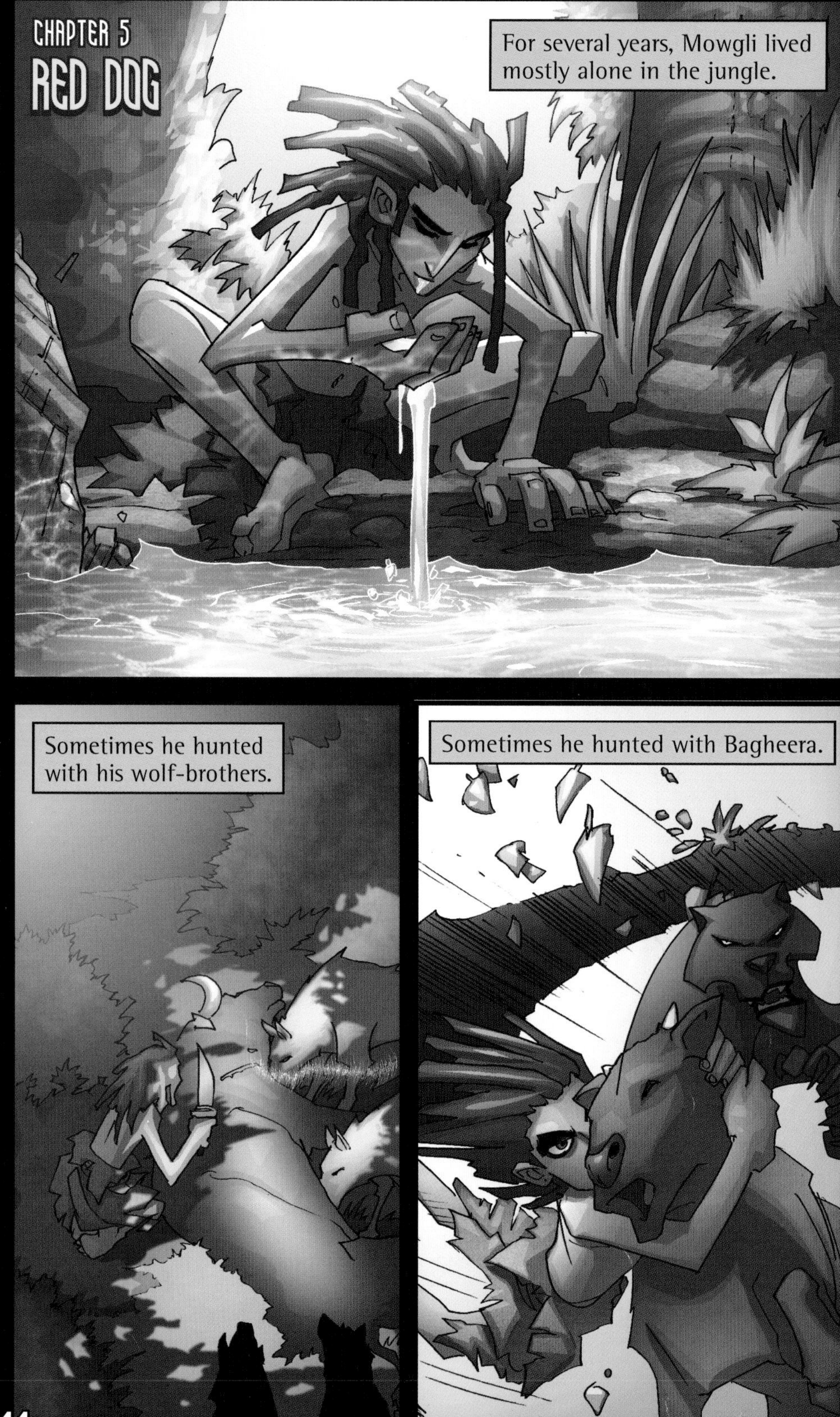
CHAPTER 5
RED DOG
For several years, Mowgli lived mostly alone in the jungle.
Sometimes he hunted with his wolf-brothers.
Sometimes he hunted with Bagheera.

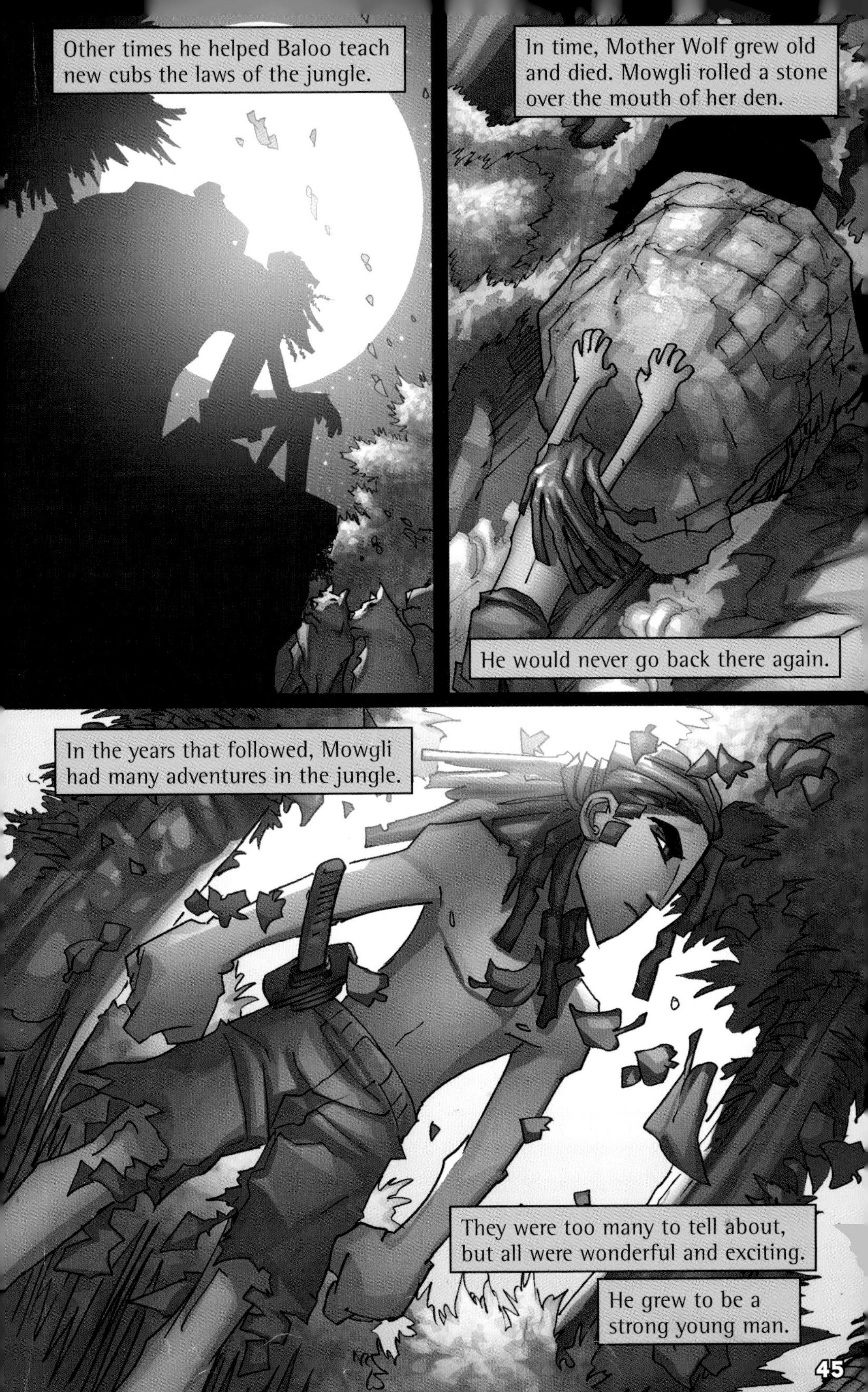
Other times he helped Baloo teach new cubs the laws of the jungle.
In time, Mother Wolf grew old and died. Mowgli rolled a stone over the mouth of her den.
He would never go back there again.
In the years that followed, Mowgli had many adventures in the jungle.
They were too many to tell about, but all were wonderful and exciting.
He grew to be a strong young man.

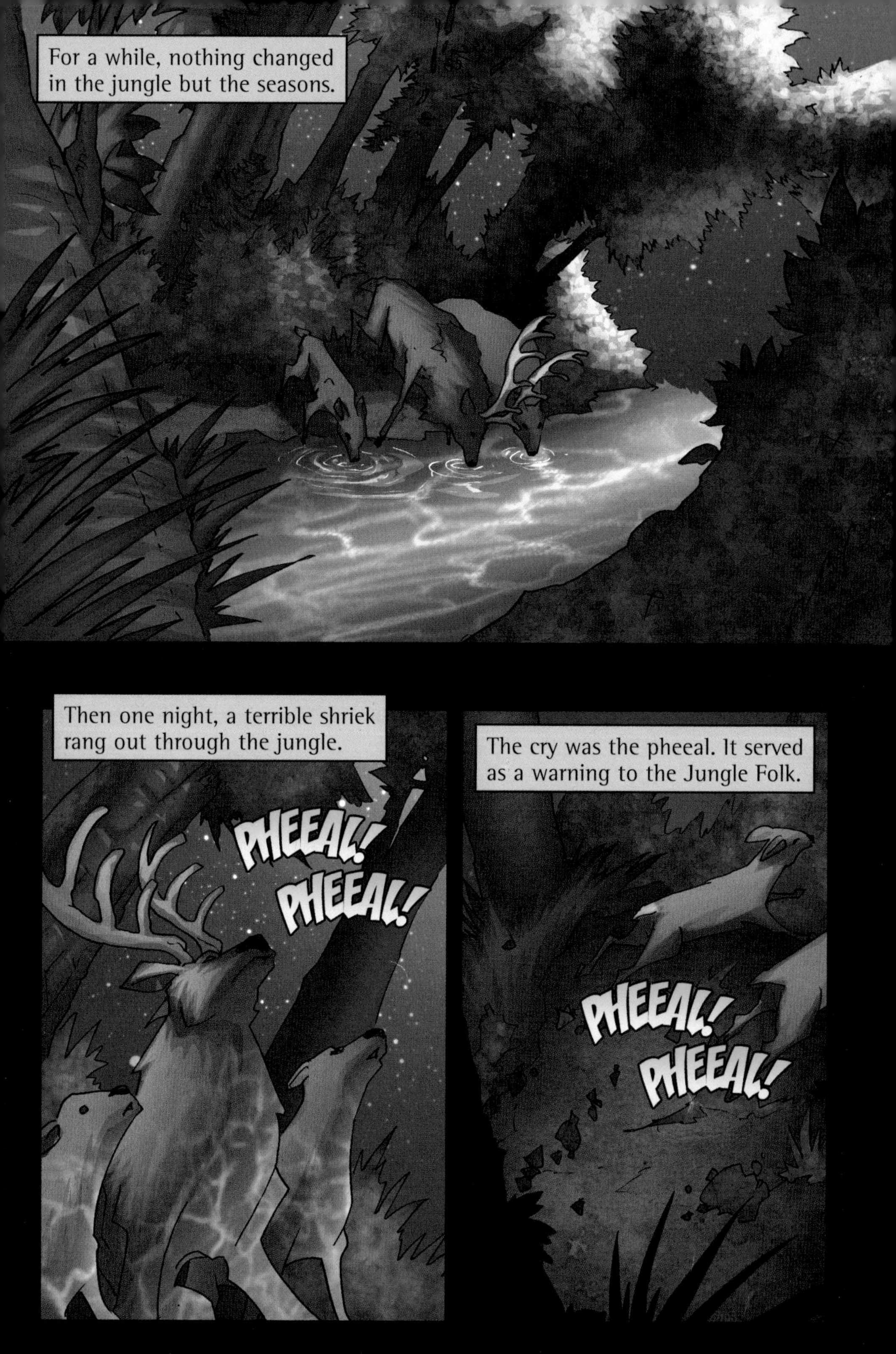
For a while, nothing changed in the jungle but the seasons.
Then one night, a terrible shriek rang out through the jungle.
PHEEAL! PHEEAL!
The cry was the pheeal. It served as a warning to the Jungle Folk.
PHEEAL! PHEEAL!

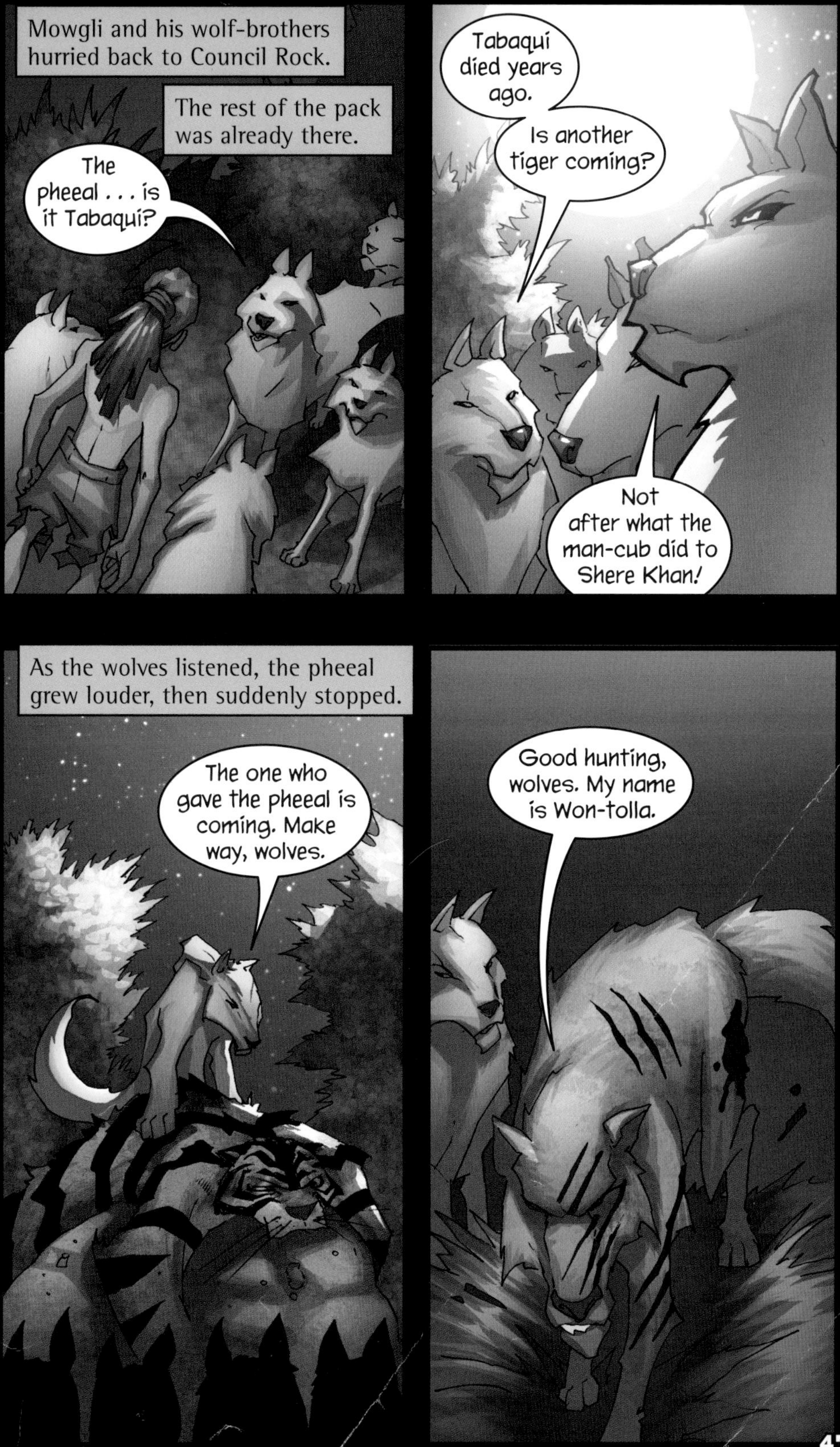
Mowgli and his wolf-brothers hurried back to Council Rock.
The rest of the pack was already there.
The pheeal . . . is it Tabaqui?
Tabaqui died years ago.
Is another tiger coming?
Not after what the man-cub did to Shere Khan!
As the wolves listened, the pheeal grew louder, then suddenly stopped.
The one who gave the pheeal is coming. Make way, wolves.
Good hunting, wolves. My name is Won-tolla.

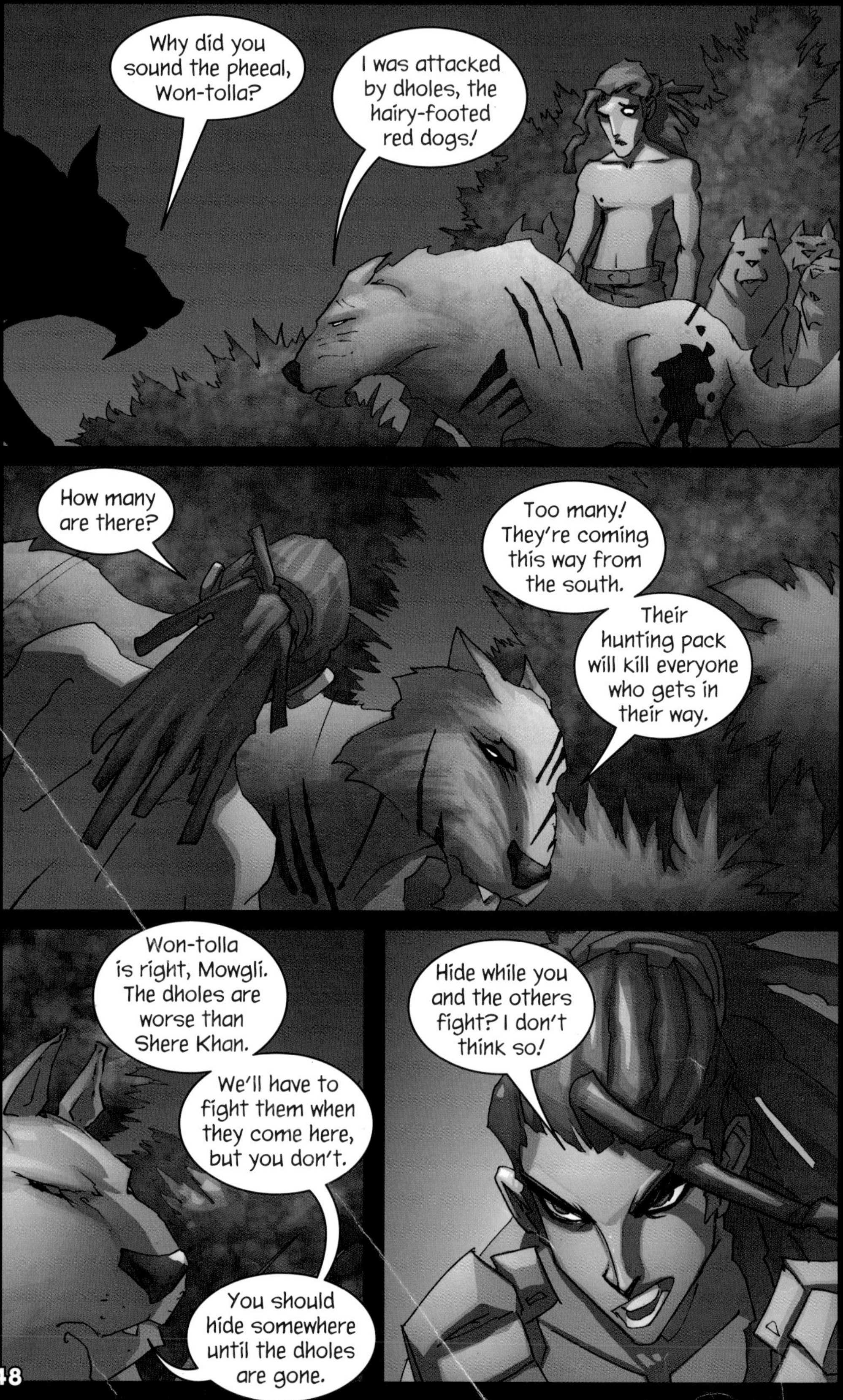
Why did you sound the pheeal, Won-tolla?
I was attacked by dholes, the hairy-footed red dogs!
How many are there?
Too many! They're coming this way from the south.
Their hunting pack will kill everyone who gets in their way.
Won-tolla is right, Mowgli. The dholes are worse than Shere Khan.
We'll have to fight them when they come here, but you don't.
You should hide somewhere until the dholes are gone.
Hide while you and the others fight? I don't think so!

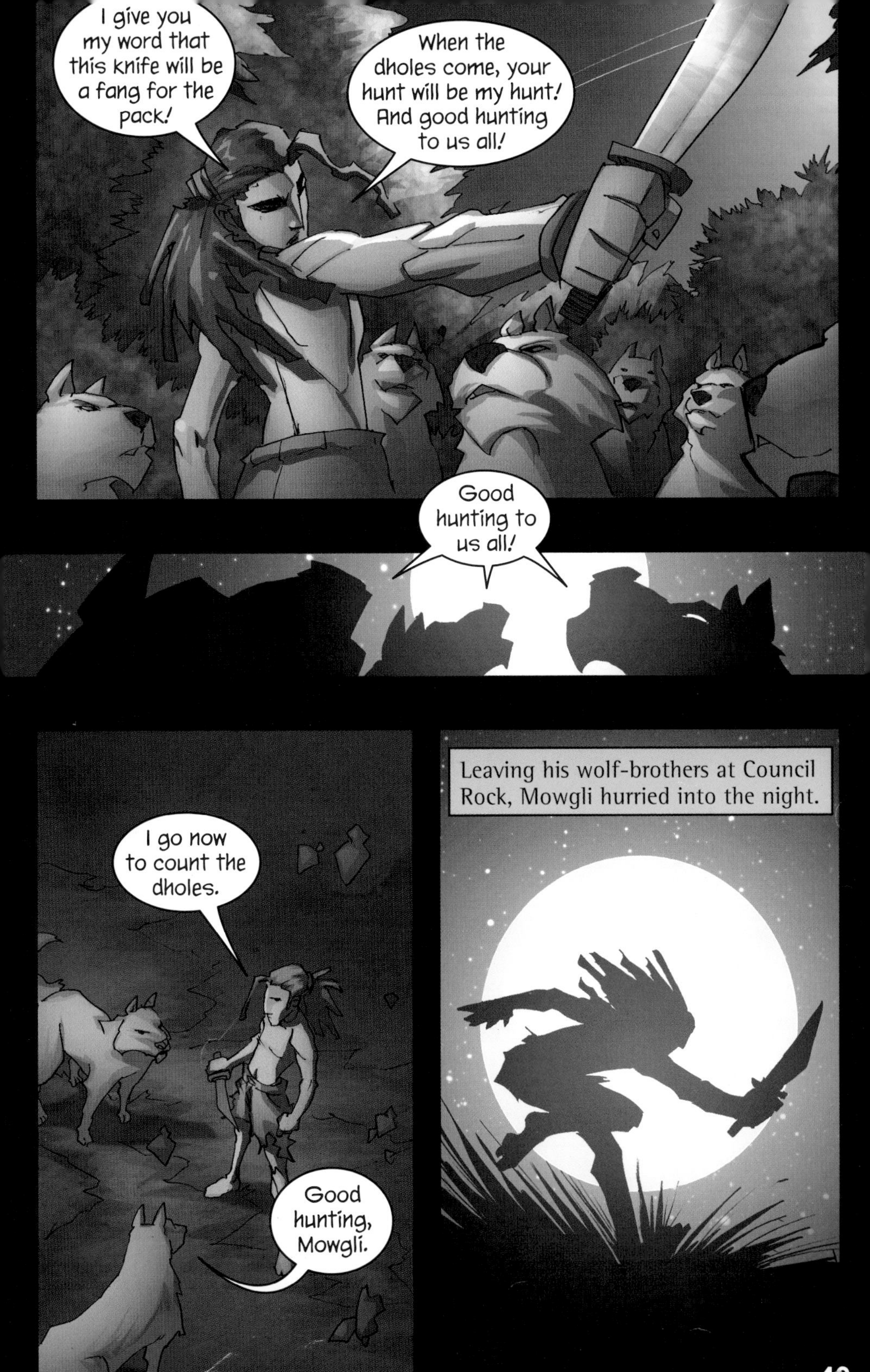
I give you my word that this knife will be a fang for the pack!
When the dholes come, your hunt will be my hunt! And good hunting to us all!
Good hunting to us all!
I go now to count the dholes.
Good hunting, Mowgli.
Leaving his wolf-brothers at Council Rock, Mowgli hurried into the night.

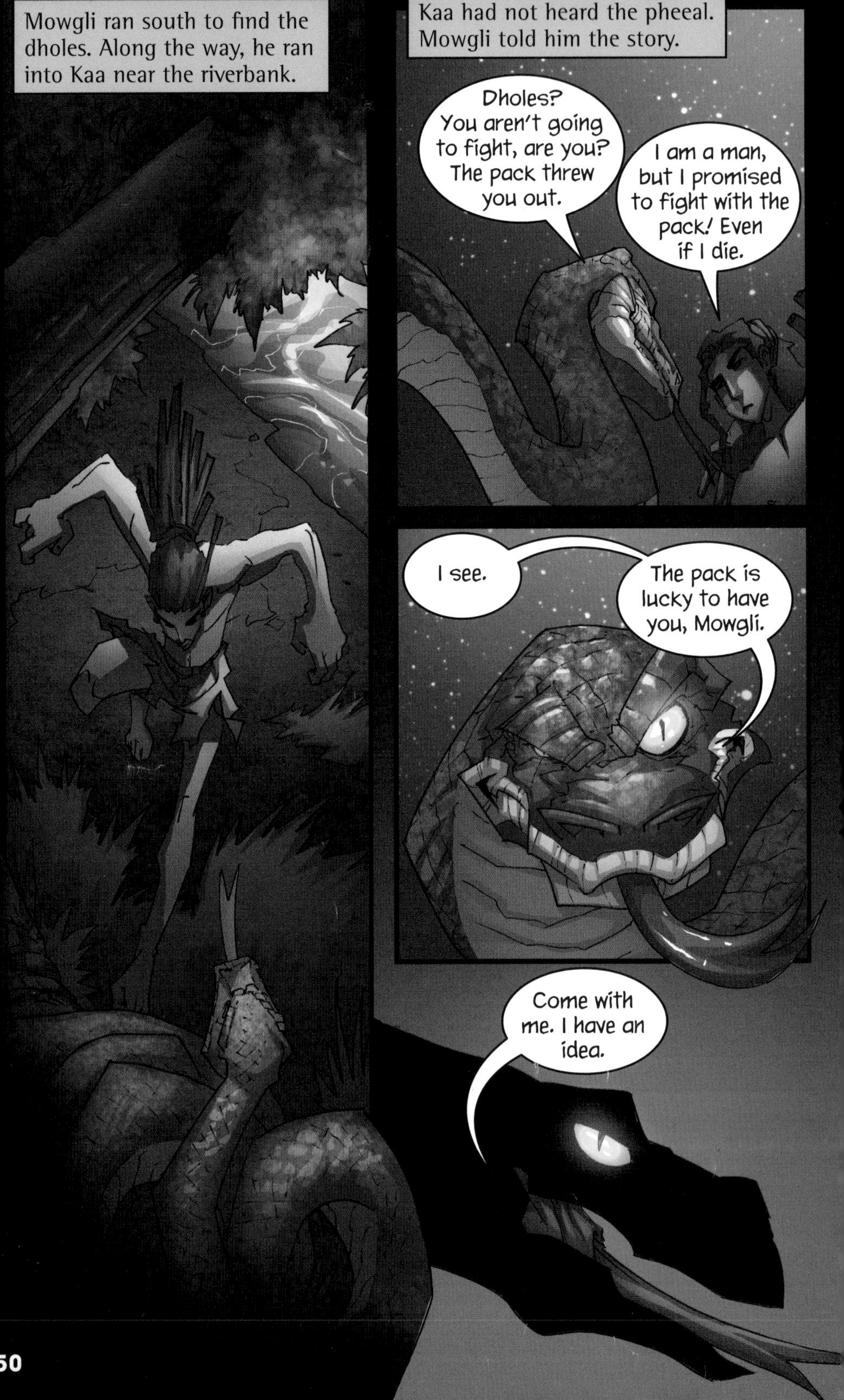
Mowgli ran south to find the dholes. Along the way, he ran into Kaa near the riverbank.
Kaa had not heard the pheeal. Mowgli told him the story.
Dholes? You aren't going to fight, are you? The pack threw you out.
I am a man, but I promised to fight with the pack! Even if I die.
I see.
The pack is lucky to have you, Mowgli.
Come with me. I have an idea.

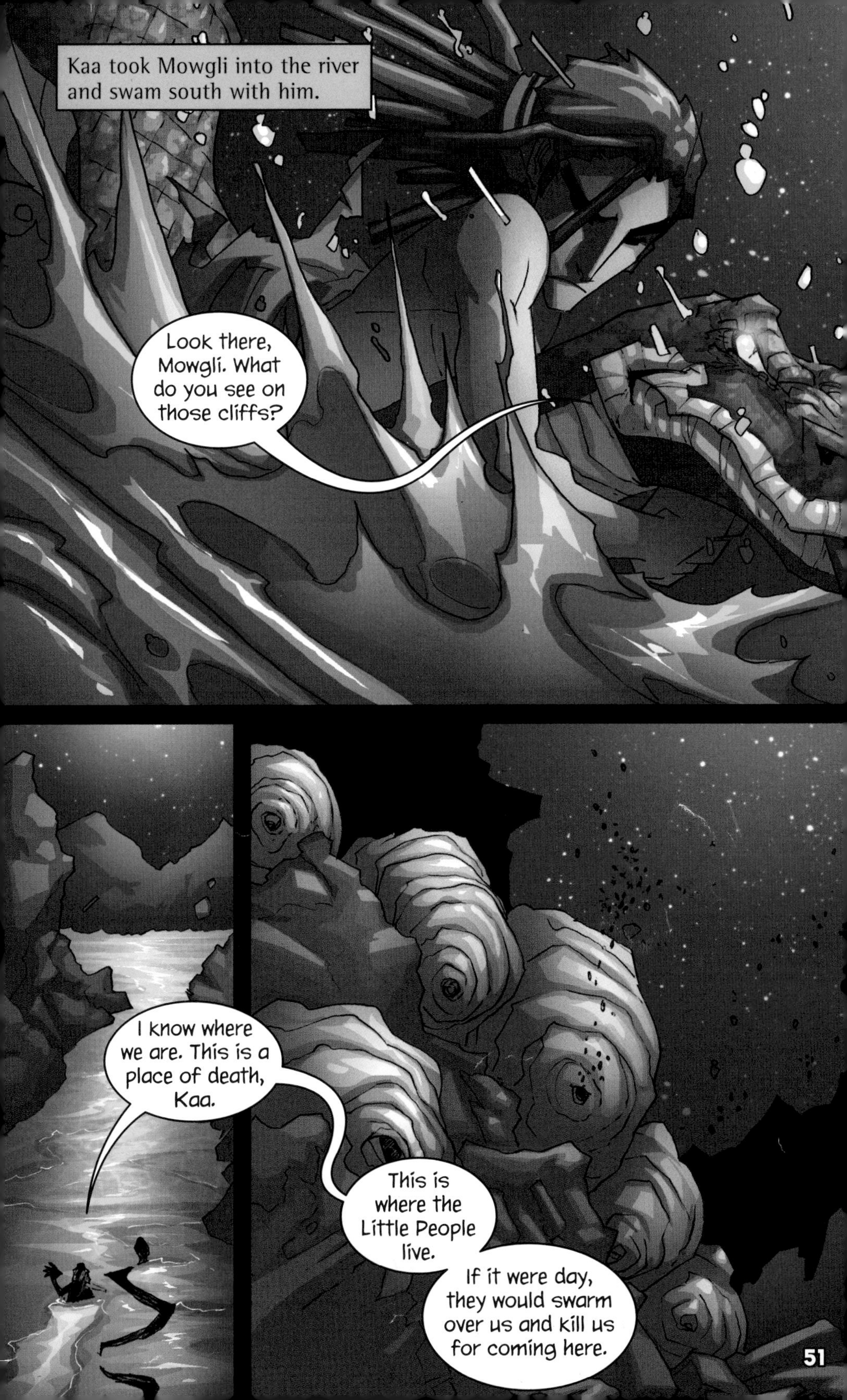

Kaa took Mowgli into the river and swam south with him.
Look there, Mowgli. What do you see on those cliffs?
I know where we are. This is a place of death, Kaa.
This is where the Little People live.
If it were day, they would swarm over us and kill us for coming here.

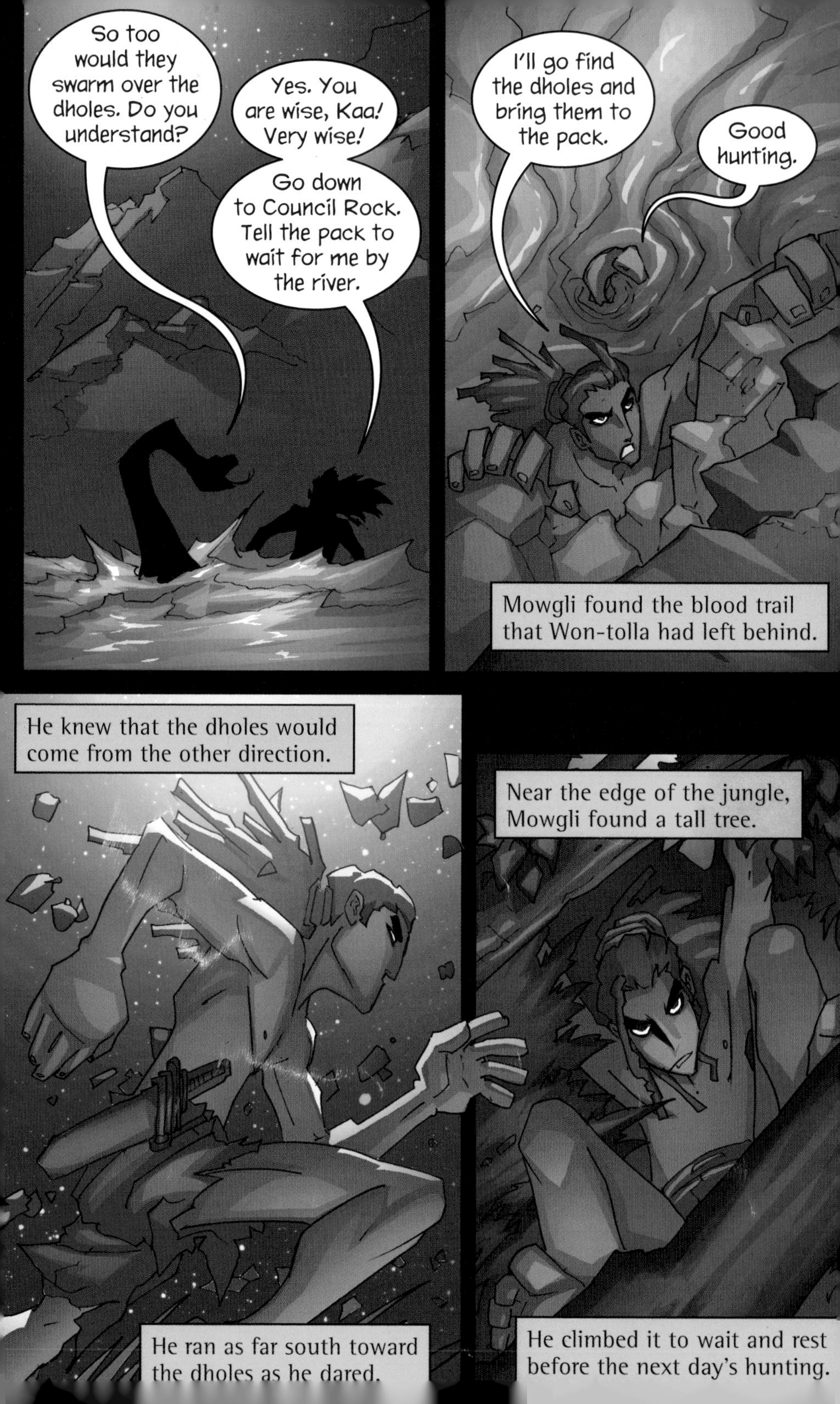
So too would they swarm over the dholes. Do you understand?
Yes. You are wise, Kaa! Very wise!
Go down to Council Rock. Tell the pack to wait for me by the river.
I'll go find the dholes and bring them to the pack.
Good hunting.
Mowgli found the blood trail that Won-tolla had left behind.
He knew that the dholes would come from the other direction.
He ran as far south toward the dholes as he dared.
Near the edge of the jungle, Mowgli found a tall tree.
He climbed it to wait and rest before the next day's hunting.

At morning, the dholes appeared, still following Won-tolla's trail.

There were more than two hundred of them.

When they reached his tree, Mowgli called out.

Run home, red dogs, if you want to live!

Come down here, hairless ape! Your jungle is our jungle now!

In answer, Mowgli taunted the dholes and called them names.

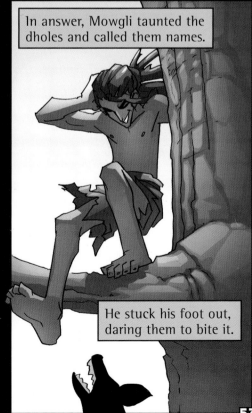

He stuck his foot out, daring them to bite it.

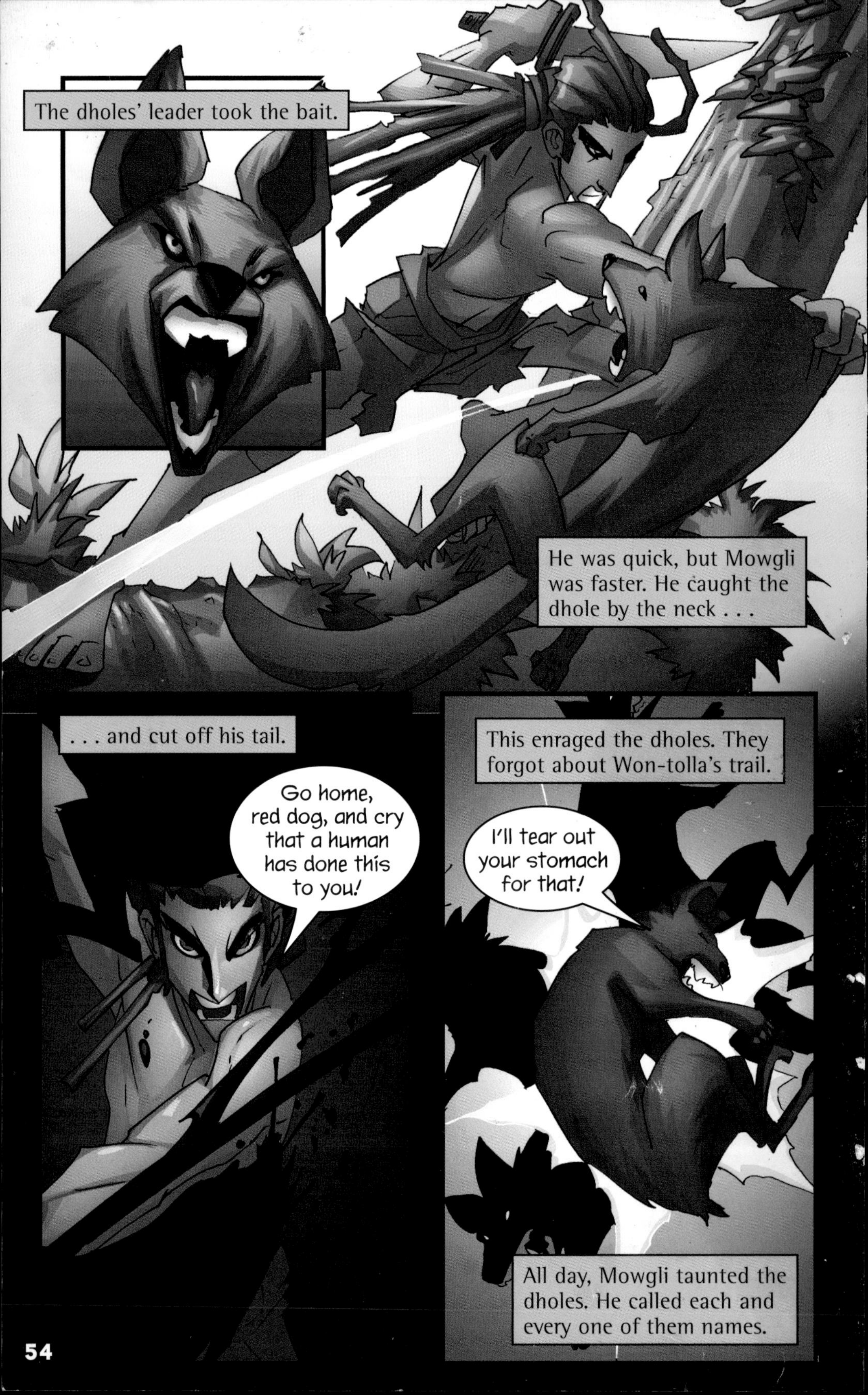
The dholes' leader took the bait.
He was quick, but Mowgli was faster. He caught the dhole by the neck . . .
. . . and cut off his tail.
Go home, red dog, and cry that a human has done this to you!
This enraged the dholes. They forgot about Won-tolla's trail.
I'll tear out your stomach for that!
All day, Mowgli taunted the dholes. He called each and every one of them names.

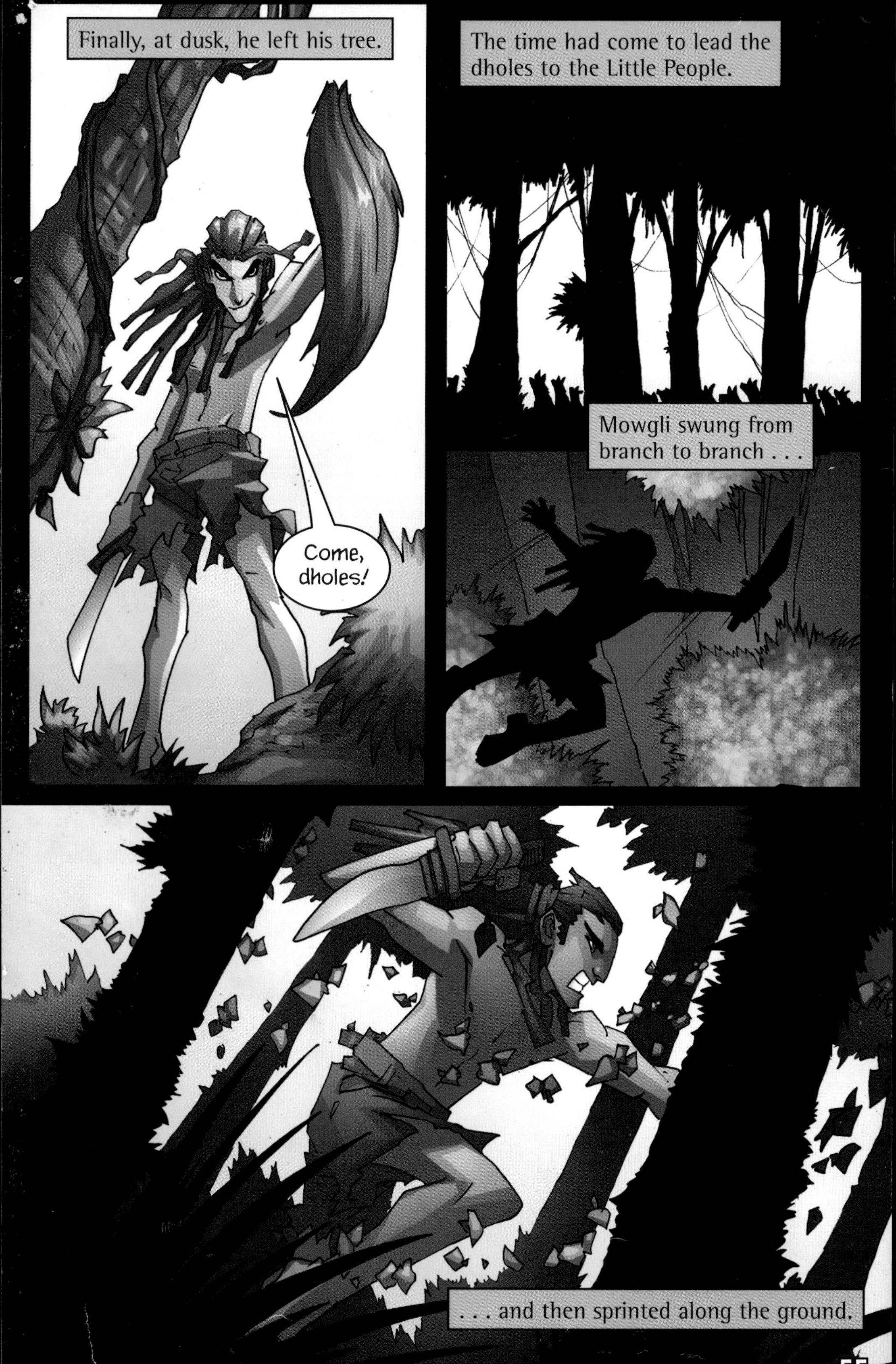
Finally, at dusk, he left his tree.
Come, dholes!
The time had come to lead the dholes to the Little People.
Mowgli swung from branch to branch . . .
. . . and then sprinted along the ground.

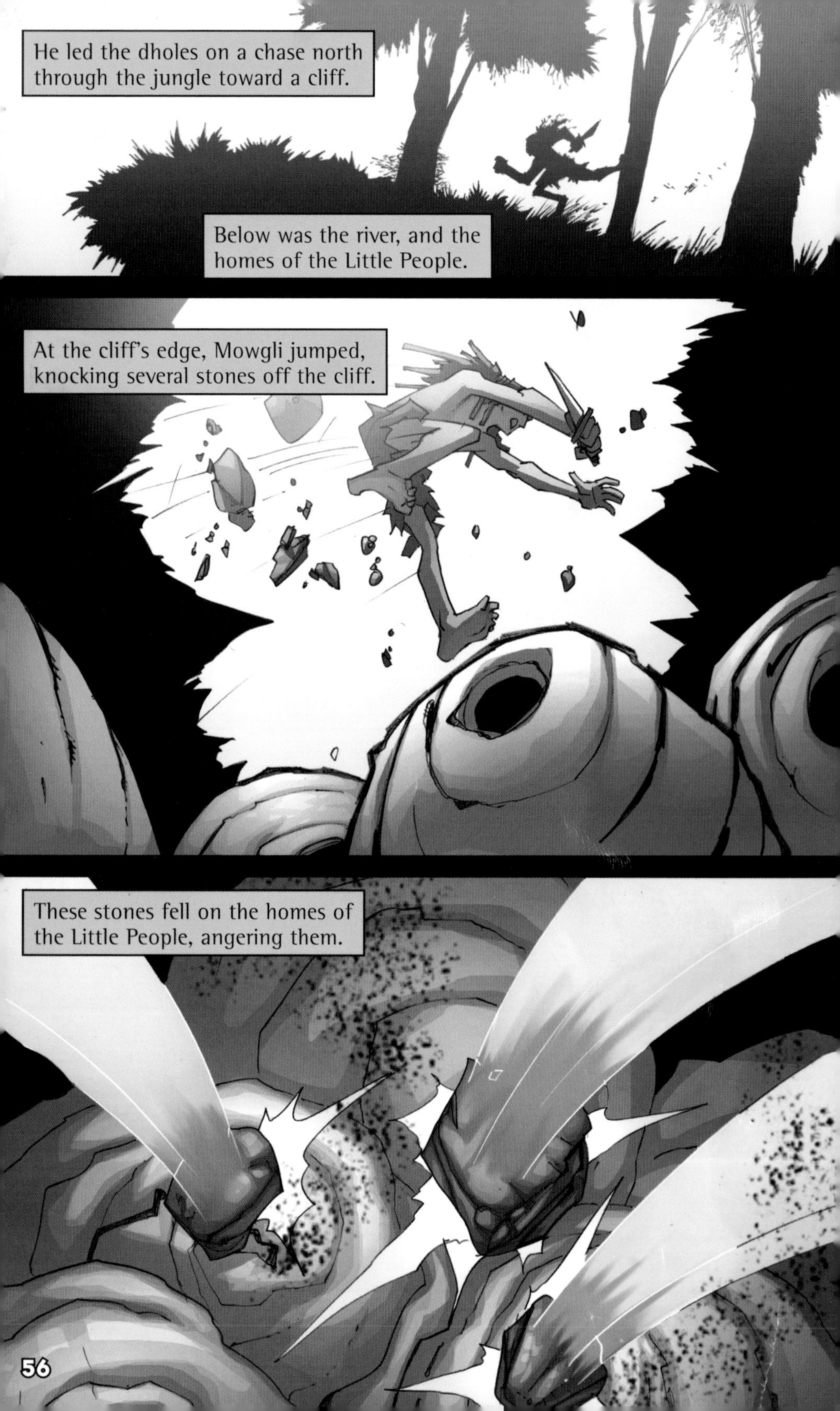
He led the dholes on a chase north through the jungle toward a cliff.
Below was the river, and the homes of the Little People.
At the cliff's edge, Mowgli jumped, knocking several stones off the cliff.
These stones fell on the homes of the Little People, angering them.

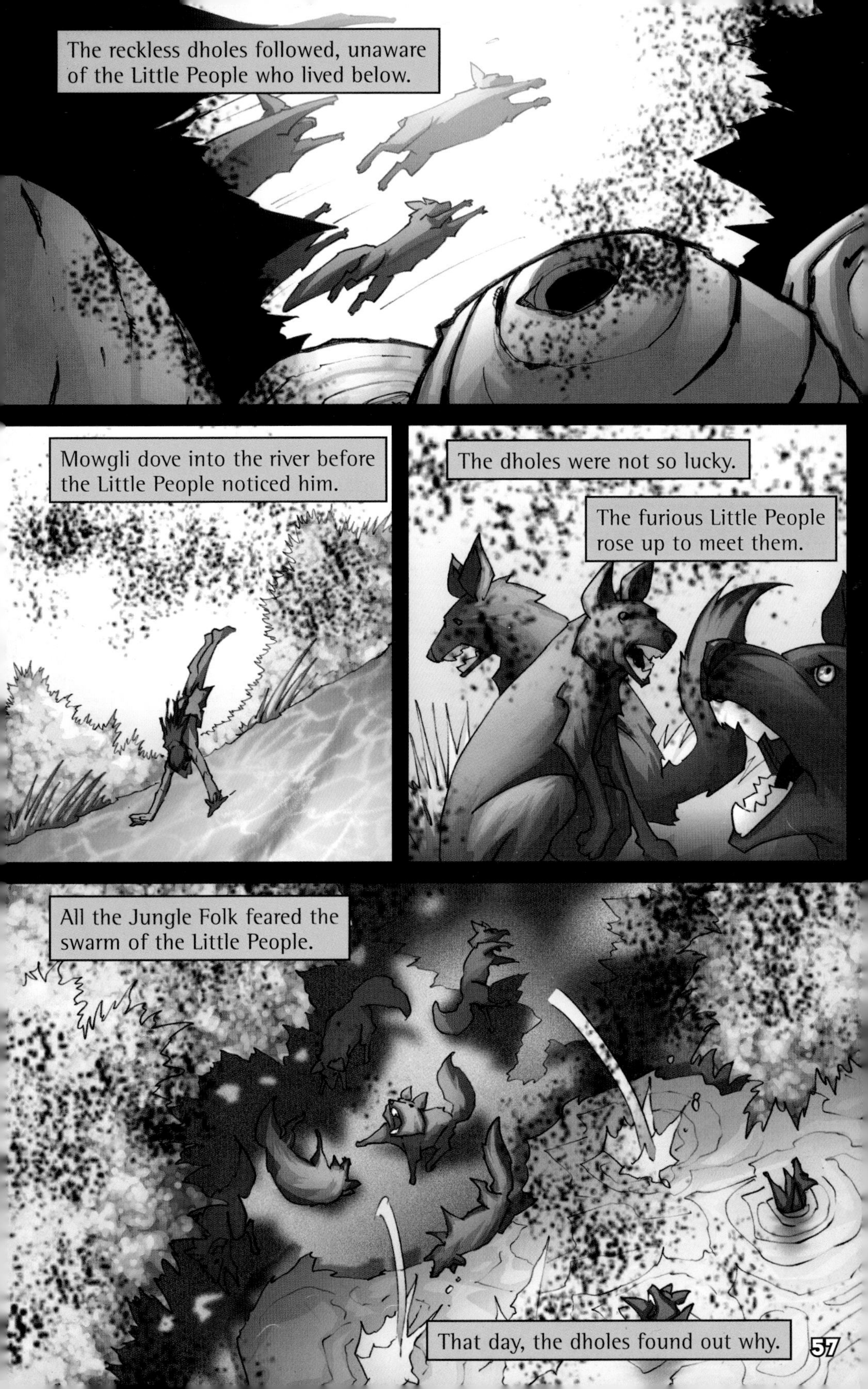
The reckless dholes followed, unaware of the Little People who lived below.
Mowgli dove into the river before the Little People noticed him.
The dholes were not so lucky.
The furious Little People rose up to meet them.
All the Jungle Folk feared the swarm of the Little People.
That day, the dholes found out why.

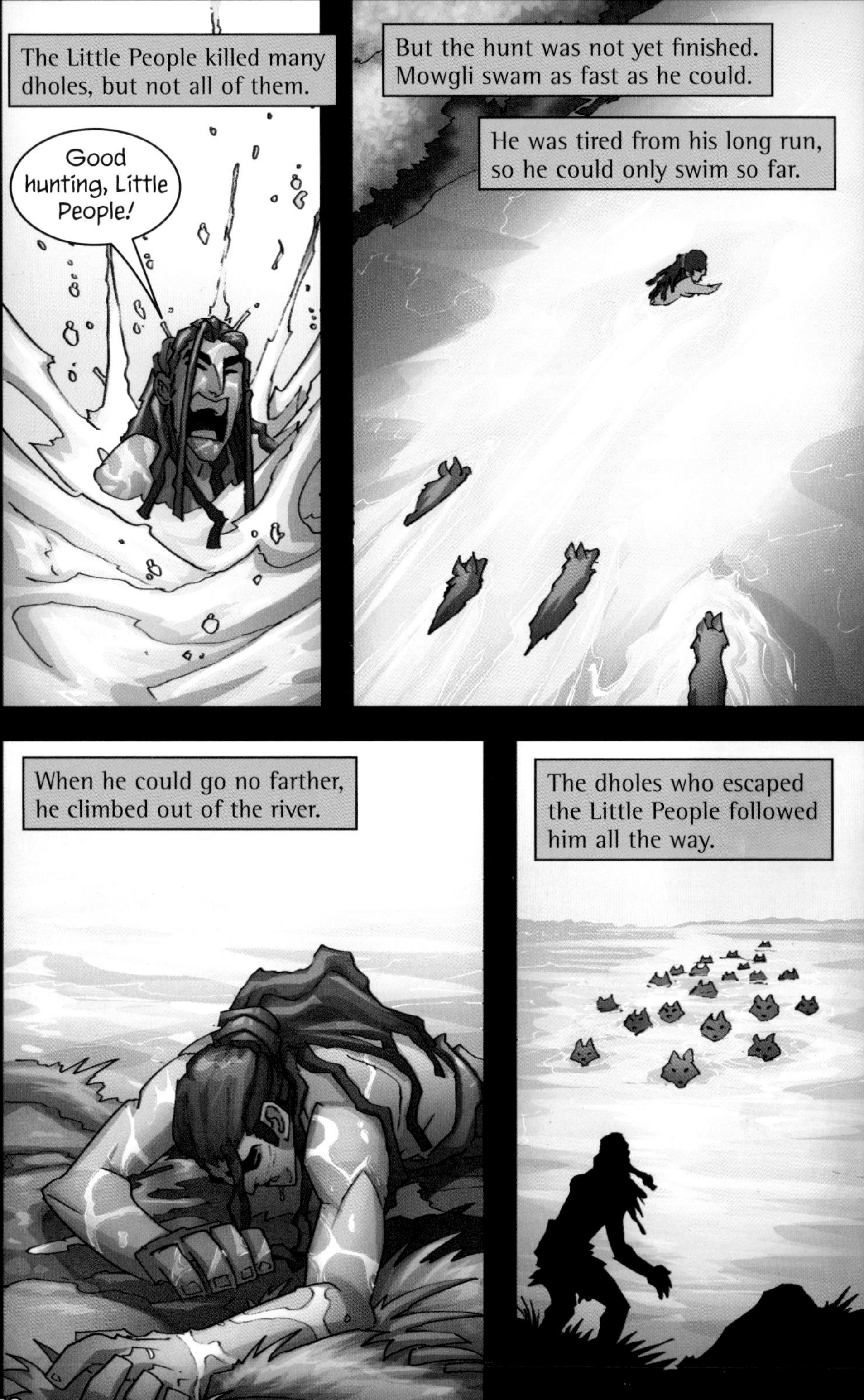
The Little People killed many dholes, but not all of them.
Good hunting, Little People!
But the hunt was not yet finished. Mowgli swam as fast as he could.
He was tired from his long run, so he could only swim so far.
When he could go no farther, he climbed out of the river.
The dholes who escaped the Little People followed him all the way.

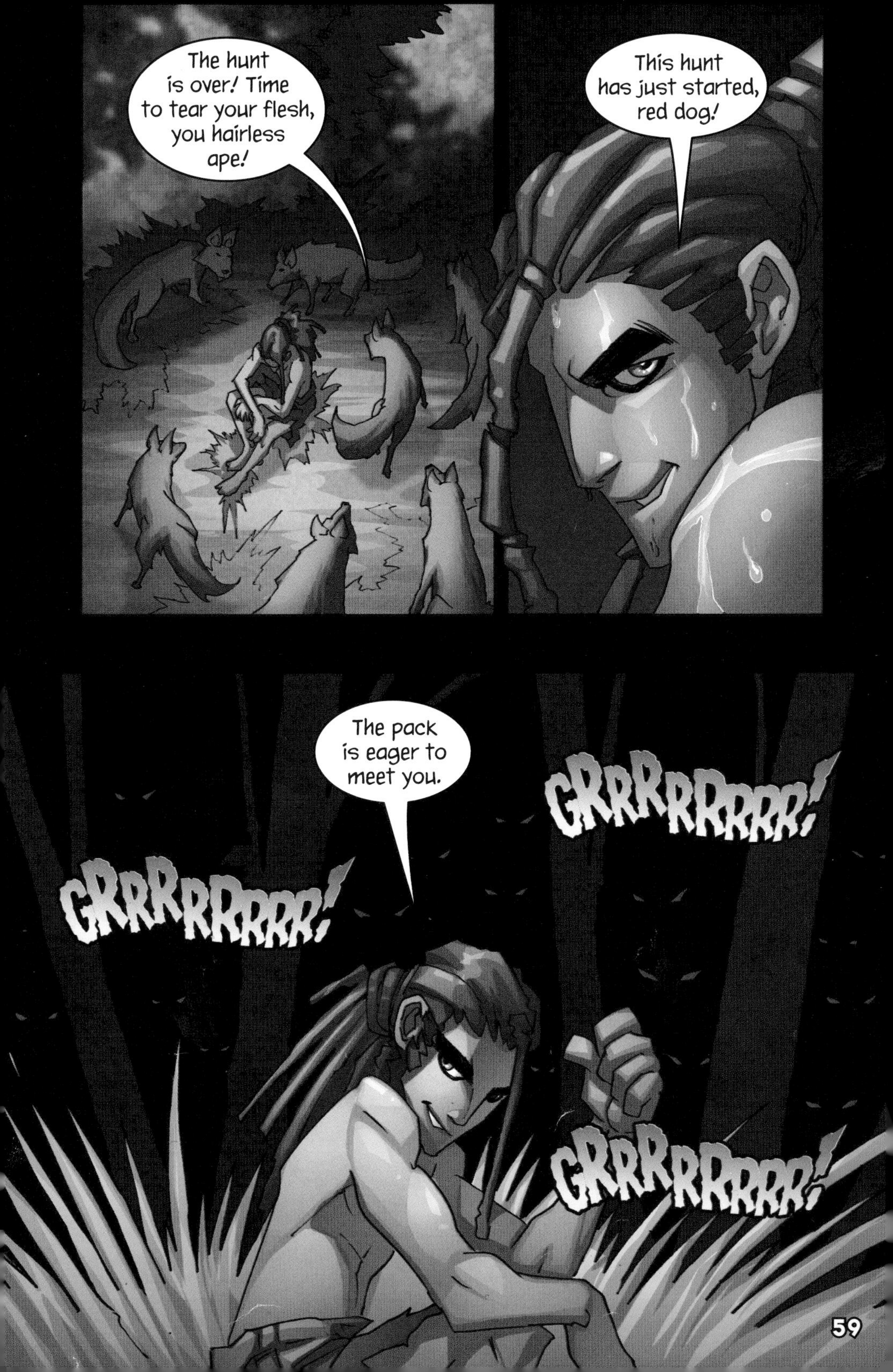

The hunt is over! Time to tear your flesh, you hairless ape!
This hunt has just started, red dog!
The pack is eager to meet you.
GRRRRRRRR!
GRRRRRRRR!
GRRRRRRRR!

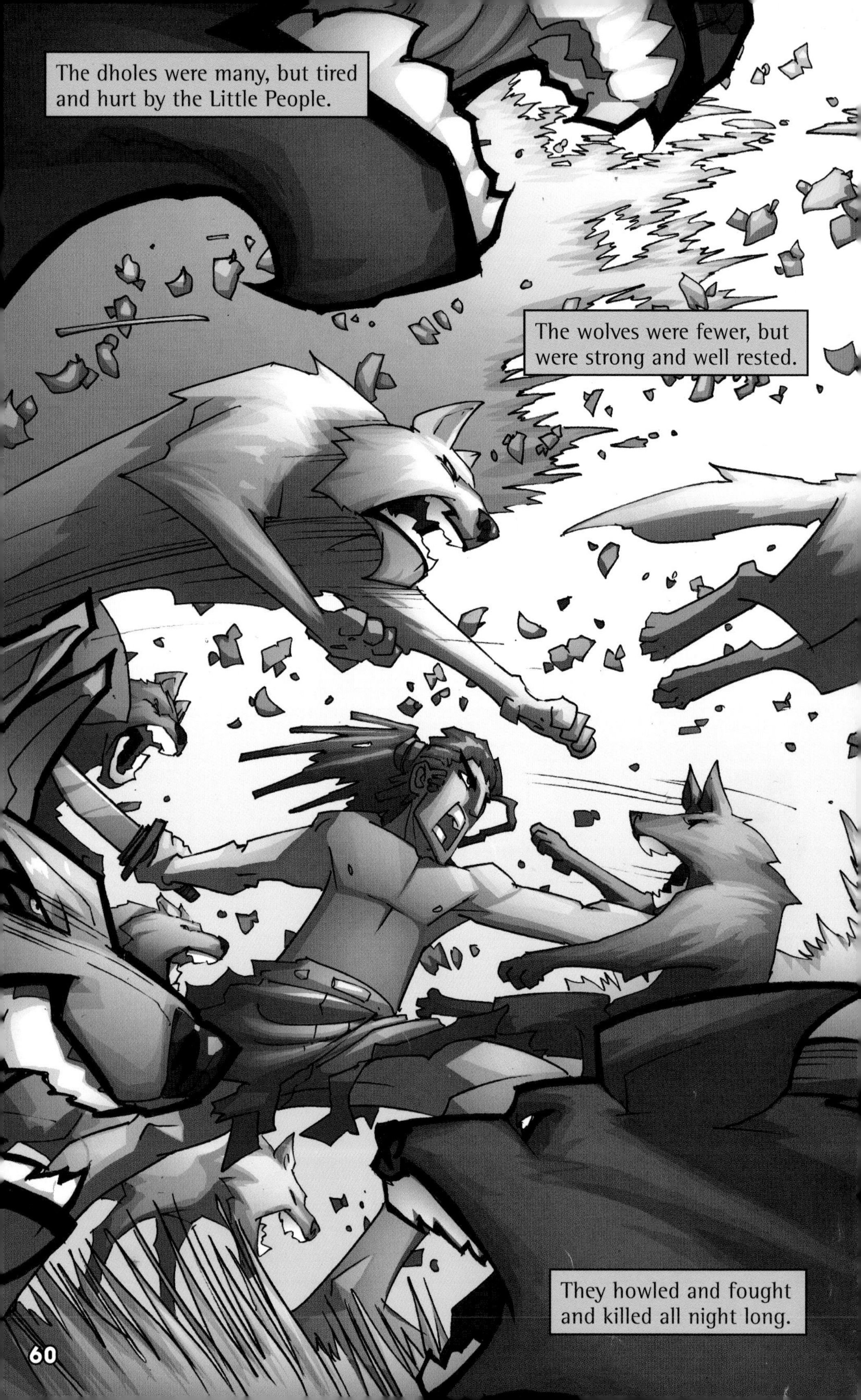
The dholes were many, but tired and hurt by the Little People.
The wolves were fewer, but were strong and well rested.
They howled and fought and killed all night long.

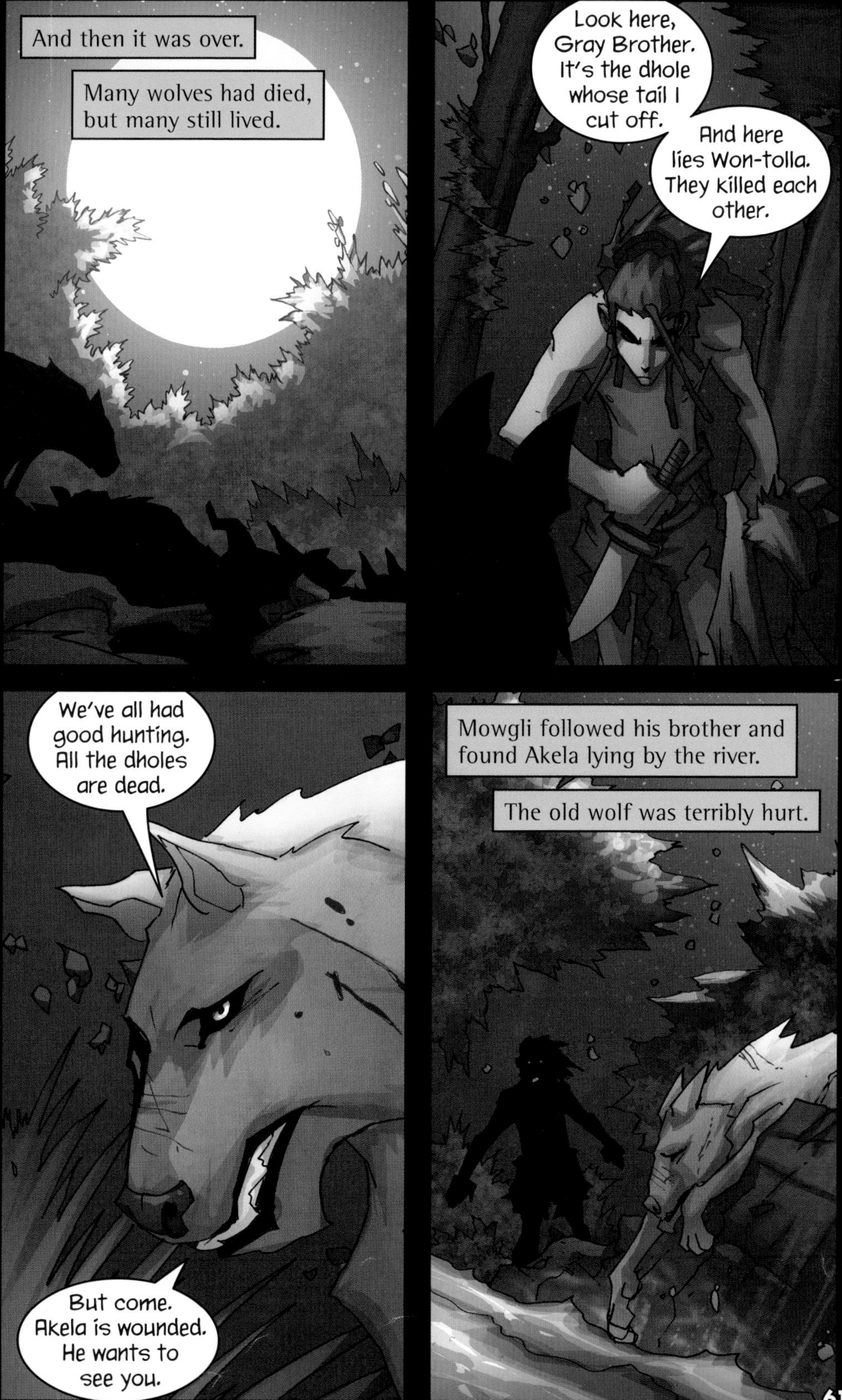

And then it was over.
Many wolves had died, but many still lived.
Look here, Gray Brother. It's the dhole whose tail I cut off.
And here lies Won-tolla. They killed each other.
We've all had good hunting. All the dholes are dead.
But come. Akela is wounded. He wants to see you.
Mowgli followed his brother and found Akela lying by the river.
The old wolf was terribly hurt.

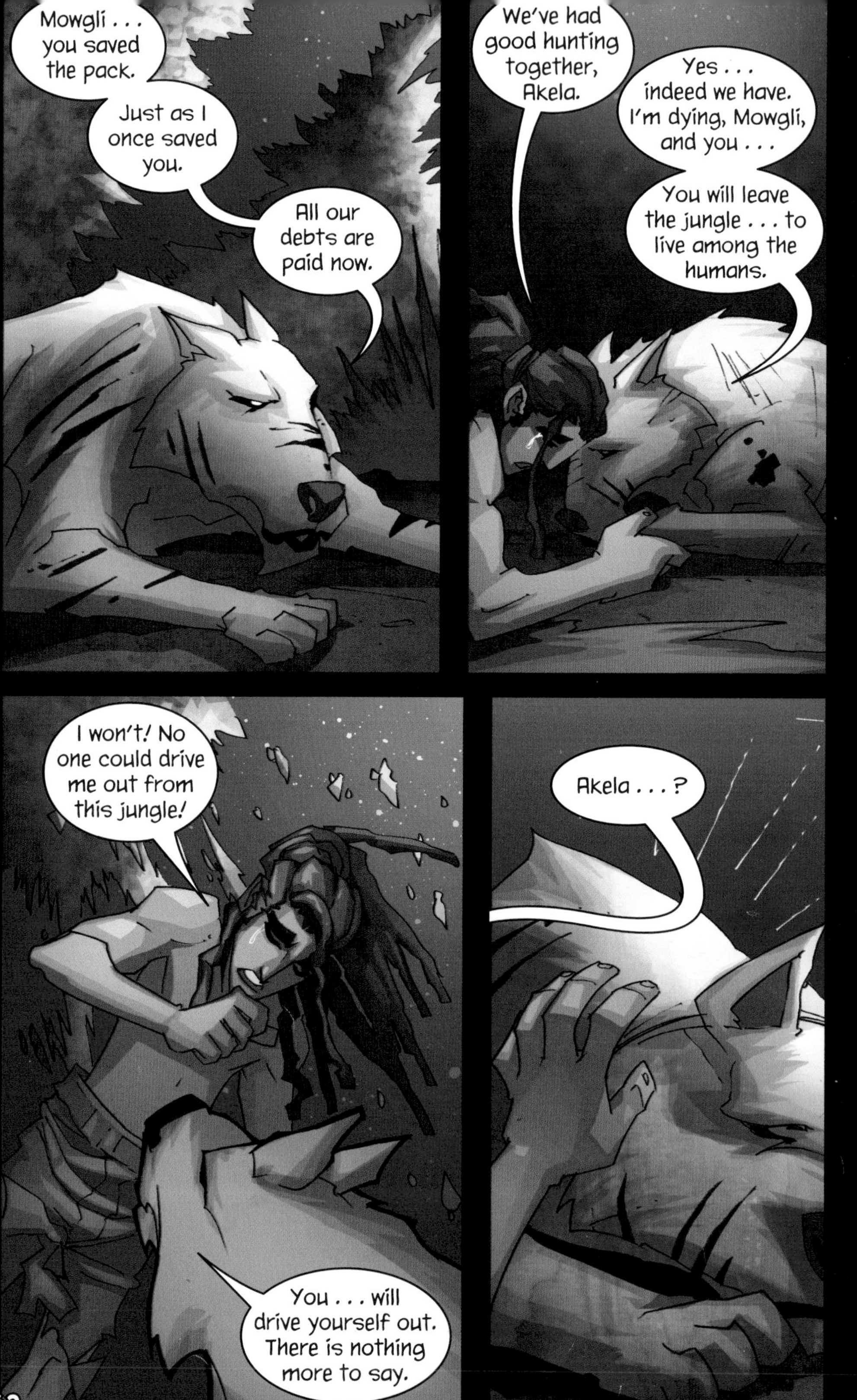
Mowgli . . . you saved the pack.
Just as I once saved you.
All our debts are paid now.
We've had good hunting together, Akela.
Yes . . . indeed we have. I'm dying, Mowgli, and you . . .
You will leave the jungle . . . to live among the humans.
I won't! No one could drive me out from this jungle!
You . . . will drive yourself out. There is nothing more to say.
Akela . . . ?

With that, Akela died, and the wolf pack howled in mourning.

Mowgli wanted to howl along with them, but he couldn't.

Akela's words troubled him. "You will leave the jungle."

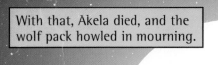

"You will drive yourself out."

Was Akela right? Would Mowgli leave the jungle to live among humans?

Maybe someday . . .

. . . but not today.

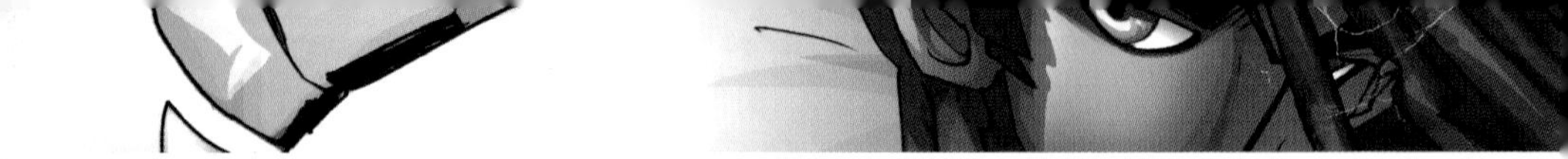

LAW OF THE JUNGLE

In 1895, a sequel to *The Jungle Book* was published. It was called *The Second Jungle Book,* and it continued the stories of Mowgli and his friends.

Inside this book is a poem called "The Law of the Jungle," which outlines a code of conduct and behavior for the Jungle Folk. Baloo would sing the poem to the wolf cubs to teach them the ways of the pack.

Now this is the Law of the Jungle — as old and as true as the sky;

And the Wolf that shall keep it may prosper, but the Wolf that shall break it must die.

As the creeper that girdles the tree-trunk, the Law runneth forward and back —

For the strength of the Pack is the Wolf, and the strength of the Wolf is the Pack.

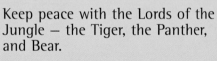

Keep peace with the Lords of the Jungle — the Tiger, the Panther, and Bear.

And trouble not Hathi the Silent, and mock not the Boar in his lair.

When Pack meets with Pack in the Jungle, and neither will go from the trail,

Lie down till the leaders have spoken — it may be fair words shall prevail.

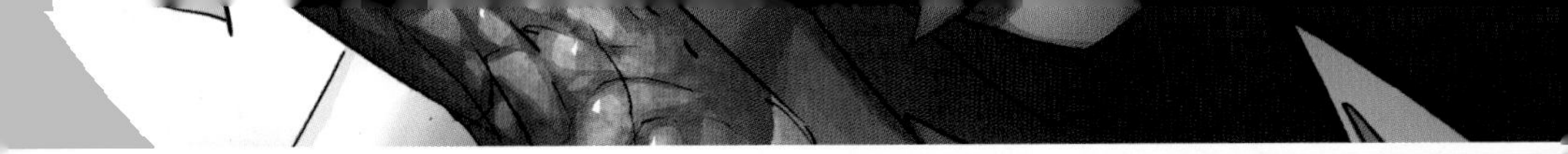

The Lair of the Wolf is his refuge, and where he has made it is home

Not even the Head Wolf may enter, not even the Council may come.

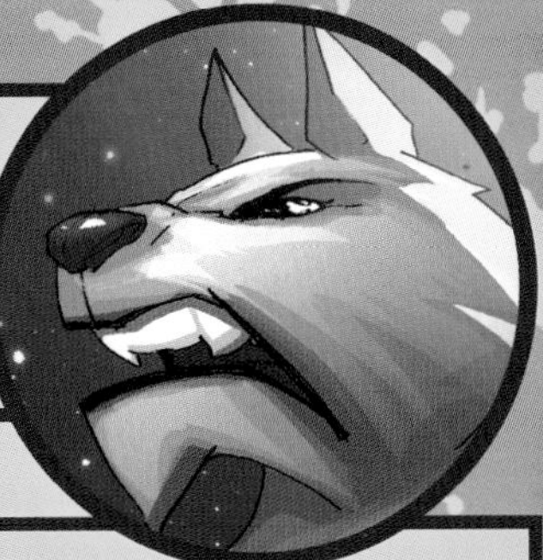

You may kill for yourselves and your mates, and your cubs as they need and you can;

But kill not for pleasure of killing, and seven times never kill Man!

The Kill of the Pack is the meat of the Pack. You must eat where it lies;

And no one may carry away of that meat to his lair, or he dies.

The Kill of the Wolf is the meat of the Wolf. He may do what he will;

But, till he has given permission, the Pack may not eat of that Kill.

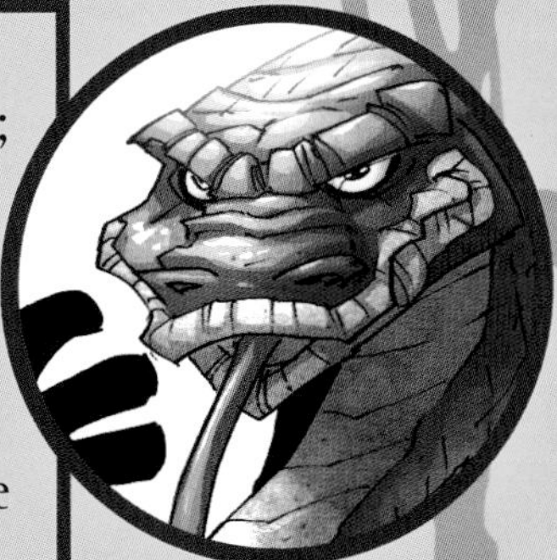

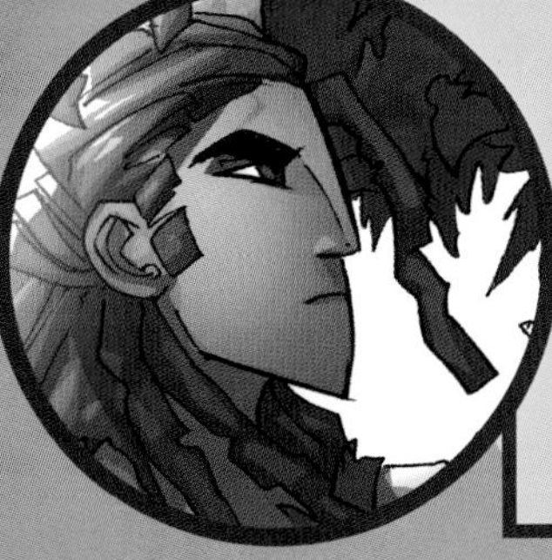

Now these are the Laws of the Jungle, and many and mighty are they;

But the head and hoof of the Law and the haunch and the hump is — OBEY!

ABOUT THE AUTHOR

Joseph Rudyard Kipling was born in Bombay, India, on December 30, 1865. He is best known for his collection of stories called *The Jungle Book*, which was published in 1894. He wrote a variety of other short stories, including "Kim" and "The Man Who Would Be King," and many poems. In 1907, he received the Nobel Prize in Literature, becoming the first English-language writer and youngest person to win the award. On January 18, 1936, he died in London at age 70.

ABOUT THE RETELLING AUTHOR

Carl Bowen is a writer and editor who lives in Lawrenceville, Georgia. He was born in Louisiana, lived briefly in England, and was raised in Georgia, where he attended grammar school, high school, and college. He has published a handful of novels and more than a dozen short stories, all while working at White Wolf Publishing as an editor and advertising copywriter. His first graphic novel is called *Exalted*.

ABOUT THE ILLUSTRATOR

Gerardo Sandoval is a professional comic book illustrator from Mexico. He has worked on many well-known comics including Tomb Raider books from Top Cow Production. He has also worked on designs for posters and card sets.

GLOSSARY

beware (bi-WAIR)—a warning to look out for something dangerous or harmful

careless (KAIR-luhss)—someone who is careless does not think things through and often makes mistakes

dared (DAIRD)—was brave enough to do something

den (DEN)—the home of a wild animal

determined (di-TUR-mihnd)—if you are determined to do something, you have made a firm decision to do it

enraged (en-RAYJD)—made someone very angry

herd (HURD)—a large group of animals that moves together as a group

mourning (MORN-ing)—being very sad and grieving for someone who has died

pack (PAK)—a group of wolves or other animals that sticks together

regret (ri-GRET)—to be sad or sorry about something

taunted (TAWNT-id)—tried to make someone angry or upset by teasing them

trampled (TRAM-puhld)—damaged or crushed something by walking over it

DISCUSSION QUESTIONS

1. Mowgli tricked the dholes into being attacked by the Little People. Is it ever okay to trick others? Why or why not?

2. Do you think it's possible for a human baby to be raised by wild animals? Explain.

3. Should Mowgli return to live with humans, or does he belong in the jungle with the pack? If you were him, which would you choose?

WRITING PROMPTS

1. When Mowgli was young, Baloo taught him many things. Which person in your life has taught you the most? What did he or she teach you? Write about it.

2. There are many interesting characters in this book. Choose your favorite character and retell your favorite part of this story from that character's perspective.

3. At the end of the book, Mowgli has not yet decided if he will stay with the pack or return to live with humans. Write a final chapter to his story that tells what Mowgli does next.

GRAPHIC NOVEL
Lewis Carroll's
Alice in
WONDERLAND
retold by Martin Powell
illustrated by Daniel Perez
CLASSIC FICTION

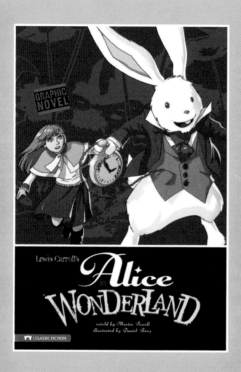

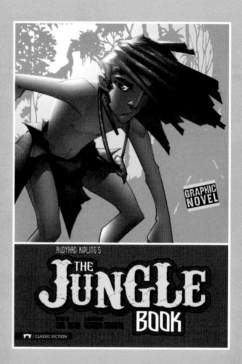

ALICE IN WONDERLAND

One day, a young girl named Alice spots a frantic White Rabbit wearing a waistcoat and carrying a pocket watch. She follows the hurried creature down a hole into the magical world of Wonderland. While there, Alice meets more crazy creatures, and plays a twisted game of croquet with the Queen of Hearts. But when the Queen turns against her, this dream-like world quickly becomes a nightmare.

GRAPHIC NOVEL
RUDYARD KIPLING'S
THE JUNGLE BOOK
CLASSIC FICTION

THE JUNGLE BOOK

In the jungles of India, a pack of wolves discover a young boy. They name the boy Mowgli and protect him against dangers, including Shere Kan, the most savage tiger in the jungle. As Mowgli grows up, he learns the ways of the jungle from Bagheera the panther, the wise bear, Baloo, and other animals. Soon, he must decide whether to remain among beasts or embrace his own kind.

CLASSICS!

GRAPHIC NOVEL
CARLO COLLODI'S
PINOCCHIO
RETOLD BY MARTIN POWELL
ILLUSTRATED BY JOSE ALFONSO OCAMPO RUIZ
CLASSIC FICTION

GRAPHIC NOVEL
L. FRANK BAUM'S
THE WIZARD OF OZ
RETOLD BY MARTIN POWELL
ILLUSTRATED BY JORGE BREAK
CLASSIC FICTION

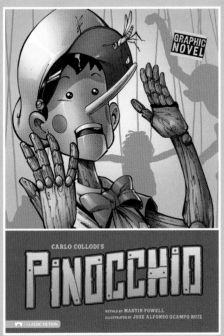

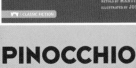

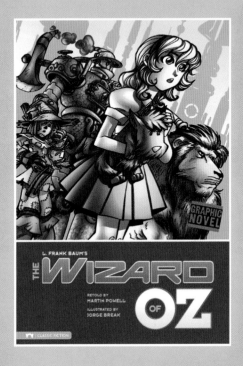

PINOCCHIO

Once upon a time, the dream of a lonely woodcutter is fulfilled when his puppet comes to life. Unfortunately, Pinocchio quickly becomes more of a prankster than a pleasure. He would rather create mischief and play tricks than keep up on his studies. Soon, however, the wooden puppet learns that being a real boy is much more complicated than simply having fun.

THE WIZARD OF OZ

On a bright summer day, a cyclone suddenly sweeps across the Kansas sky. A young girl named Dorothy and her dog, Toto, are carried up into the terrible storm. Far, far away, they crash down in a strange land called Oz. To return home, Dorothy must travel to the Emerald City and meet the all-powerful Wizard of Oz. But the journey won't be easy, and she'll need the help of a few good friends.

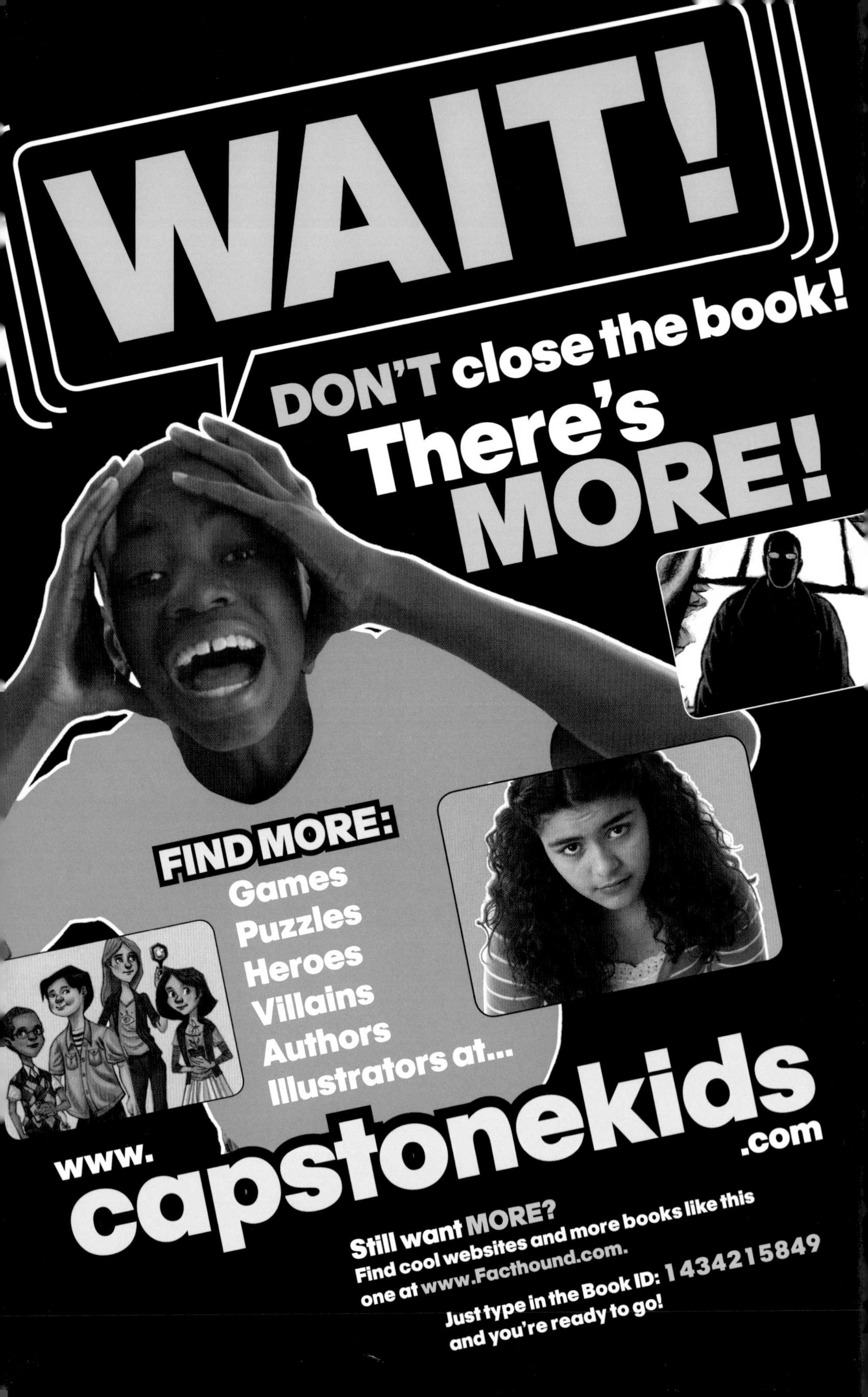
WAIT!
DON'T close the book!
There's MORE!
FIND MORE:
Games
Puzzles
Heroes
Villains
Authors
Illustrators at...
www.capstonekids.com
Still want MORE?
Find cool websites and more books like this one at www.Facthound.com.
Just type in the Book ID: 1434215849
and you're ready to go!